SAVAGES

SINISTER GRIN PRESS

SAVAGES

GREG F. GIFUNE

SINISTER GRIN PRESS
MMXVI
AUSTIN, TEXAS

Sinister Grin Press Austin, TX
www.sinistergrinpress.com
September 2016

Cover Art by Zach McCain
Text Design by Brian Cartwright

My sincere thanks to Matt Worthington and everyone at

SINISTER GRIN PRESS.

This one's for Dave Thomas.

"A man cannot destroy the savage in him by denying its impulses. The only way to get rid of temptation is to yield to it…"

—*Dr. Jekyll and Mr. Hyde* (1920 film)

AFTER

Flames slashed the darkness. It looked as if the whole world was on fire, and in a way, it was. Spreading rapidly, the flames attached to and burned everything in their path, lighting up the trees and brush as showers of sparks shot high into the air, cascading back to earth with a majesty reserved for those things both beautiful and deadly. This destroyer, burning with furious violence, surged through the night like the seductress it was, and despite a misty rain blowing in off an otherwise calm sea, the fire continued to gain power and momentum, engulfing everything in its brilliant agony.

But the raging fire was not the only predator here. The other, newly ordained, crouched and waited, mesmerized by the inferno. Nude and concealed in the small pockets of remaining darkness, skin covered in wounds, blood and soot, only the whites of the eyes were visible, wide and alive and teeming with ravenous, primal ferocity. When it finally moved, it was with astonishing newfound stealth, confidently slinking through the fiery night, its movements fluid, efficient and lethal. The heat from the blaze flushed its face, caused its eyes to water and burn. Unmoved, it watched the flames through blurred vision. Discomfort—*pain*—was part of it now, something to embrace, dominate and master, rather than fear.

The fire, so vast and powerful that its radiance illuminated nearly the entire island, would burn for hours yet, and perhaps even here, at the ends of the earth, someone might see the flames and come to investigate.

Or perhaps not.

Perhaps there was no rescue from this hell, no escape. Perhaps there never had been. Perhaps it no longer mattered because things were no longer the same. *It* was no longer the same. It feared it was no longer fully human, that it had become something else. Something less.

Rising from its haunches, the phantom surveyed the carnage with peculiar satisfaction.

Wake up, a voice deep within it whispered. *Wake up*.

But there would be no awakening, not from this.

It turned and darted into the burning, white-hot jungle, just like the beast of prey it had become.

CHAPTER ONE

His mind told him it was only a game, and for a brief moment he was a child again, playing at the beach, lying in the wet sand at the very edge of the ocean's reach after a long swim. Always a fan of adventure stories and movies, Dallas remembered pretending he was a fearless hero fighting the bad guy at water's edge, or struggling to survive against the elements, pirates or deadly sharks in the open ocean. Sometimes he was the lone survivor of a shipwreck who had washed ashore on a desert isle, and he'd lie on the beach then crawl his way to drier sand, exhausted but alive. As those fantasies and memories flooded his mind for the first time in ages, all in vivid detail, the irony was not lost on him, particularly as he rolled lifelessly with the surf, turning and moving through the ocean with the push of each new wave. How could he have known all those years ago as a little boy that his favorite playtime scenario would one day become horrifyingly real?

His world was still dark and blurred, so either his vision hadn't yet returned and he wasn't totally conscious, or he'd been knocked out and was coming around while still being tossed about the ocean in the dead of night. Either way, he was reasonably sure he was still in the water, but close to shore of some kind, because his body scraped a rocky bottom, and for the first time in a while, Dallas felt pain, spikes of it shooting up through his ribcage and into the base of his throat. He tasted saltwater and blood, gagged then felt himself moving of his own accord. Flailing, actually, before collapsing into thick wet sand, his fingers sinking deep beneath its surface, clutching at the earth with everything he had, which suddenly was quite a lot. Pushing and kicking with his legs, he managed to propel himself up and forward before flopping onto his belly in what felt like a spray of dry sand.

I'm on land, he thought. *I'm…alive…I—my God, I—I'm on land!*

He tasted grains of sand in his mouth, scraping his teeth and tickling his tongue, felt them prickling his cheeks and scratching his eyes. Far as he could tell the pain hadn't subsided, but the sensation of motion had left him, as had the tightness in his chest, the shortness of breath and the sensation of drowning. But before he could give any of that much thought, something in the surrounding darkness once again pulled him down into a well of blackness and despair.

As it took him, Dallas could only hope and pray he really had reached land—impossible as that seemed given the circumstances—and that the sensations he'd experienced weren't tricks of the mind meant to distract him while the ocean swallowed and dragged him to depths he could never escape. Perhaps what he'd felt were simply the hallucinations of a dying mind. If so, then he was still out in the middle of the ocean amidst a surging tempest and probably already dead. But if this was real, he might have a chance. A slim chance, but a chance nonetheless.

His eyes blinked. Scratchy with sand and burning from the saltwater, Dallas was cognizant of sight now, but badly blurred vision coupled with the pitch-black night left him violently dizzy. He pushed with his hands, felt soft but solid ground beneath his palms. He coughed and vomited a gush of seawater then slipped once again into unconsciousness, or something similar.

There, in the dark.

Dreams of violent struggle shriek at him from the darkness, his body writhing and kicking in blind panic as all sense of direction is lost. Beneath the ocean surface, submerged in an endless maze of water, pressure pushing him down and all sound reduced to eerie echoes and groans, he forces his eyes open despite the sting and frantically searches for a way out. And then just as suddenly, he breaks the surface, his body thrown up and out, inconsequential and useless as the other bits of debris in the water with him. He tries to scream for help but manages only a strangled croak as, without mercy, seawater surges into his mouth and down his throat. Fighting the powerful waves and crashing ocean, he tries to gain some sense of perspective, but he is lost in the night, in the storm and the raging sea, a top spinning out of control, swallowing seawater one moment and gasping for air the next. No up or down, no forward or back—nothing—just a world of water and darkness devouring him, pulling at him, slapping him down as wind rings in his ears and distant sounds of thunder growl in the night.

He dreams of the lightning too. Jagged spears unlike any he's seen before, so brilliant and enormous it looks like a special effect from some Hollywood blockbuster. It splits the black sky with great crackling forks, and he is grateful, because now he knows where the sky is, what is above him and what is surely below. But his lungs continue to struggle and he still cannot draw sufficient air. The ocean is absorbing him, filling him. He and it are becoming one. The strong devouring the weak. I'm dying, he thinks. I'm about to die, violently, in this place and on this night.

Sometime later, the water brought him around. Or perhaps it was the sun. He couldn't be sure which and didn't much care. He only knew he was awake, and therefore, alive. And as he raised his head from the hot sand and squinted against the unexpected brightness of daylight, Dallas also realized that the night before was no dream. It was real, all of it. The boat really had gone down in a storm. He and the others abandoned ship, and all but one of them, a crewman named Davis, made it to the raft. Eight people total, only six fit safely in the raft, which meant at all times two had to float alongside, holding on. Though the captain was injured and couldn't be moved, the others alternated, surviving the blistering days and seemingly endless nights as best they could. For three days and nights they drifted in the Pacific. They saw no signs of land, no planes or rescue ships. And then another storm hit and the raft capsized. Dallas was sure he'd died, but he was alive and really *had* washed ashore somewhere.

With a grunt he attempted to move his fingers, and then his

hands and arms. His muscles were stiff and sore, but he had a fairly decent range of motion. Next he tried his toes and feet, and eventually his legs. Again, there were sore muscles but apparently no serious injuries. But when he tried to rise up onto his hands and knees using a pseudo pushup motion, the pain from the prior night returned. Harsh and sharp, it tore across his chest from deep inside. His lungs burned and stabbing pain rifled across his chest and up into his shoulders and neck. He'd slammed into something solid with his chest and could only hope nothing was broken or busted up inside. He drew a breath, shallow at first, and then a bit deeper. By the time he'd taken a full breath the pain was excruciating. He'd had pneumonia several years before, and though he knew that's not what this was, it felt similar. He coughed. His throat and chest burned. Ignoring it as best he could, Dallas crawled, dragging himself further up the beach. Exhausted, he flipped onto his back and lay there a moment, breathing heavily despite the pain.

The canopy of cloudless sky above him was a brilliant shade of blue. He turned his head and spat, but it did little to lessen the sandy grit and muck coating his mouth. It tasted like he'd swallowed half the ocean floor and then gargled the other half. He wiped his mouth and face with his forearm and spat again. For days he'd struggled with hunger and thirst as he and the others rationed what little food and water they had as best they could, and now the idea of eating or drinking anything made him sick to his stomach.

In time he worked his way into a sitting position but was still too dizzy to stand, so he stayed put and took in his surroundings as his mind slowly focused. He was on a small island, likely uninhabited, yet he still had the desire to scream for help. He didn't have the wind, so instead he sat quietly and listened to the ocean waves gently lap shore mere inches from where the current had deposited him the night before. Had he remained there much longer, the tide would've eventually swept him back out to sea. He hugged himself at the thought then inspected his body for injuries. He was wearing only a pair of khaki shorts. He didn't even have shoes on. He, like the others, had already been badly sunburned and littered with blisters, but now his feet were lashed with tiny cuts and scrapes, as were his knees, elbows, arms, shoulders and chest, no doubt from the way he'd bounced in along the rocky coastline, pushed there by the storm and left to tumble to shore like a ragdoll. Like his blisters, the cuts, contusions and scrapes were numerous, but none were life-threatening.

Shielding his eyes with his hand, he gazed out at the beach and ocean beyond. The water was crystal clear, the sand white and hot. He turned, looked back over his shoulder. Several yards of beach led to a small embankment sprinkled with numerous palm trees. Perhaps another forty yards from the first trees there stood a second band, and then jungle. Dallas forced a swallow, coughed then turned and groggily looked to his right to find a fairly long stretch of beach and more palm trees dotting the embankment in that direction as well. To his left he saw rocks, lots of large dark jagged monstrosities protruding from the surf like ancient stone totems. Had he approached the island from that direction he'd have washed ashore in pieces.

In the distance, in a small cove near the far end of the island, something out of place on the white sand caught his attention. He watched it a while to make sure it wasn't a trick of the glaring sun. A patch of yellow material was strewn across the sand, part of it still in the water and moving gracefully with the sway of the ocean. He rubbed his eyes and looked again. It was definitely there, no question. Dallas stared at it for what seemed a very long time, waiting for his mind to catch up. When it finally did he struggled to his feet, and although his legs were shaky and he was still a bit lightheaded, he staggered along the shoreline fast as he could toward the remains of what he now recognized as the rubber life raft. *The others*, he thought. *They made it too, they—please don't let me be the only one!*

Quinn's face drifted past his mind's eye.

My God, Quinn! Where the hell is she? Is she all right?

Trauma had stolen his memories of Quinn and the others, and now that he'd regained them they flooded his mind in a furious and uncontrollable montage. Chest aching, head pounding, his body weak and his feet burning on the hot sand, Dallas staggered along the beach beneath the harsh sunshine, unable to think of anything now but Quinn and the others.

He stumbled twice but kept on without falling, and as he closed on the cove he angled closer to the water and slowed his pace. When he reached moist sand he carefully crawled over a cluster of large rocks then dropped down to the other side.

Swaying but still upright, breathless and dripping with perspiration, he again found the remains of the inflatable raft. It was flat, tangled and shredded in several places, and a modest plastic paddle was still attached to one section by a thin piece of white nylon rope. While the rear section remained in shallow water, the rest of the destroyed raft had been washed ashore.

Dallas stumbled closer and dropped to his knees.

There was no sign of Quinn or anyone else.

He closed his eyes as his throat constricted. The awful thirst was back.

"Quinn!" The scream was louder than he'd thought himself capable of, so he called her name again and again with as much fury as he could muster.

There was no answer.

In time his calls became a horrible weeping sob, her name mangled by his cries of rage and fear, confusion and frustration. He desperately clutched a scrap of raft with both hands and held it to his chest as the world blurred through tears.

After a moment his body slumped and he fell silent, kneeling in the wet sand.

When he heard what sounded like a disembodied voice beckoning him from very far away, Dallas assumed he'd slipped back into unconsciousness and the realm of nightmares.

But the voice not only persisted, it grew louder, closer.

He raised his head, pawed tears and sand from his eyes and looked to the far side of the cove. Through the bright sun came a figure, running and stumbling along the waterline, arms waving. Calling him— the figure was calling him—and he knew that voice, knew who it was even before her face came into view.

"Quinn?" he asked softly, his voice raspy and labored but laced with hope.

Fighting his exhausted and battered body, Dallas struggled to his feet and headed toward the figure. The prospect of having lost his wife once had nearly destroyed him, if this was a dream or turned out to be some cruel trick, he'd never recover.

They collided, a frenzied bundle of limbs and torsos clutching at each other and spinning, collapsing down into the sand together as both ran their hands over the other to be certain they were real and intact and as they'd remembered them. Their cracked lips met and both spoke but neither was really listening.

"Quinn! God—Quinn, I—"

"I thought I'd lost you, baby, I thought—"

"Are you all right?"

"I've been looking for you, I—"

"I'm here." He pulled her to him again and hugged her tight. "I'm here, it—it's okay, I'm right here. You're alive, my God, you—you're alive."

"I love you." Quinn kissed his neck and cheek on the way to his lips.

"Love you too, I—I love you too."

Out of breath, they sat in the sand awhile, hugging quietly, thankfully, and allowing their raw emotions to run roughshod.

Dallas looked her over more closely. Barefoot like him, she was dressed in faded nylon shorts and a bikini top. Her hair, light brown and short, was mussed and wet and caked with sand in places, and she was traumatized and as exhausted and blistered as he was, but otherwise seemed unharmed. In fact, but for the golden-brown tan she'd sported days before that had largely since turned scarlet and sunburned, she looked remarkably strong considering everything they'd been through. Thin and lithe, hers was the sinewy body of an athlete, and even at thirty-four she'd lost nothing of the lean but powerful swimmer's build she'd had when they'd first met in college and Quinn was a star member of the swim team. "You're okay?"

She nodded, cupped his face with her hands. "Are you?"

"I'm thirsty—and starving—but I'll be all right."

"You're all scratched up."

"I'm fine." He grabbed her wrist, pulled her hand to his mouth and kissed it. "What about the others?"

"Everyone's here." Quinn stole a glance back over her shoulder. "Except…"

He looked at her fearfully.

"Andre," she finally said. "No one's seen him."

The horrors of the night before and hellish days preceding it were gradually coming back to Dallas in flashes. Murdock, the captain and owner of the vessel, had been injured just before they'd abandoned ship. Dallas remembered jumping into the water after the raft along with the others, and how once it inflated they'd all made for it. Davis, the lone crewman, was the only one who'd come up missing. They all screamed and searched for him as best they could, but to no avail. He never made it off the boat.

When the storm cleared they drifted in that little raft for three days, until another squall rolled in and they'd all been thrown to the sea. Andre and Natalie had been taking their turns outside the raft when the storm hit. How in God's name any of them had survived and made land was nothing short of a miracle.

Dallas gazed out at the ocean he'd once found so beautiful. Now it was little more to him than a predator. "And the others?" he asked softly.

"They're just beyond the rocks. We've been here since last night when we made shore."

"Is everyone all right?" he asked.

She held his hands. Tight. "There's a reef." Quinn pointed out at the ocean. "There. That's what we hit last night in the storm, what threw us all from the raft. In the dark we had no idea how close to land we actually were. Murdock's still blind. His eyes are in terrible shape and he nearly drowned, but he's alive. Nat hit the rocks coming in pretty hard. She's hurt."

"Badly?"

Quinn's tears of joy were replaced with those of sorrow. "It's not good, Dallas."

"Shit," he said, regaining his feet and pulling her up with him. "Where the hell are we? Does anyone know?"

"We're not sure."

"Murdoch doesn't have any idea?"

"We were hoping he might know but he's been in and out of consciousness all night. He's in bad shape too, but it's Nat I'm worried about. Her arm's broken. I managed to set the bone, but she's got internal injuries too." Quinn's voice broke. She pulled herself back together quickly. "Nat's in terrible pain and she's coughing up blood."

"Jesus."

"Yeah," she said, wiping her eyes. "Come on."

Arms around each other, they started for the others.

They crossed the sand together, and the farther they went the stronger Dallas felt. Just knowing Quinn was alive and uninjured was enough to keep him going. She'd be strong—she always was—and he needed to be too.

Dallas saw Herm watching them as they approached. Sitting a few feet away was Harper, and on the sand between them, Nat lie quietly, Murdoch next to her.

"Holy shit," Herm said, wandering closer. He held his fist out, and purely from habit, Dallas bumped it. "You all right, man?"

"I'm alive. You okay?"

Of everyone, it was perhaps the most curious that Herm had survived. He was forty-six, which, with the exception of Murdoch, made him the oldest member of the group, and was by far in the worst shape physically. Of average height, he was a bit chubby around the waist and was the only one among them wearing long pants, or what was left of them. His jeans had been ripped and torn along both legs, but he had on a relatively intact short-sleeved white undershirt and a pair of inexpensive sneakers. Having lost his hair in his thirties, Herm wore an awful hairpiece that, although not in the best condition, had somehow managed to stay on his head throughout their ordeal. Even his eyeglasses, the kind with lenses that turned dark in sunlight, bent and scratched, were still intact. A coworker and primarily a friend of Dallas's, Herm didn't know the others well, and had been something of an awkward addition to their vacation.

Dallas looked around. "Where's Gino?"

"He went that way," Herm said, pointing listlessly toward the jungle. "He's doing his Tarzan routine, I guess. Or whoever the hell he thinks he is."

Harper, Gino's latest girlfriend and the youngest of them at only twenty-three, sat in the sand a few feet away, weeping quietly. Though her heavy makeup and false eyelashes had long since washed away, in sneakers and a little white bikini, she still had the look of a displaced stripper, her peroxide-blonde hair long and tangled to her shoulders, her busty, cartoon-like body barely contained in her skimpy swimsuit. Sitting there crying in the sand she finally looked her age, Dallas thought, even younger somehow, like a child.

He looked to Quinn. She gave a quick nod indicating Harper was upset but fine.

Dallas crouched down next to Murdoch and gently touched his wrist.

"Who's that?" he asked in a gravelly voice. "Who's there?"

"It's Dallas."

The captain of the yacht they'd booked for an overnight fishing cruise, John Murdoch, a grizzled man in his fifties, lay on his back, his dashing good looks ruined by damage the sun had caused and the bloody wounds about his eyes. When the first storm that took down the boat had hit, a rogue wave had taken out the bridge, shattering everything and raining glass and debris directly into his face. Though blinded, he'd managed to make it overboard, where the others had saved him and gotten him safely into the raft. Since then he'd been in and out of consciousness, and Quinn had done her best to tend to his wounds, but he'd been able to offer very little information, as even when he was awake, he was rarely coherent.

"John," Dallas said, "listen to me, okay, I—I need you to listen to me."

The captain turned his head toward Dallas and nodded, his eyes a bloody mess.

"Do you have any idea where we are?"

"It's not possible."

"What isn't?"

"Where we were, where we are, there—there's no land out here."

"You don't understand. Try to focus if you can, John. We're on an island."

"No, *you* don't understand," he said, his speech slurred. "There are no islands out here. There's nothing but ocean between the southernmost Cook Islands and Antarctica."

"Then where the hell are we?"

"No land, there's…no land out here…"

As Murdoch drifted back into unconsciousness, Dallas glanced at the others, but no one was making eye contact. He crawled over to Natalie, doing his best to not notice her mangled arm. Andre's girlfriend, he and Quinn and Gino had been friends for years, and he'd never seen her afflicted with anything worse than a head cold. Natalie was the den mother, the one who looked out and cared for everyone else. It seemed impossible for her to be laying there so damaged and broken, but there she was.

"Careful," Quinn warned. "Don't move her."

With a nod, Dallas took her limp hands in his. "Nat?"

She was unconscious, her chest barely rising and falling.

Quinn put a hand on his shoulder and gave it a gentle squeeze. When he looked up at her she slowly shook her head in the negative. Natalie was dying. It was only a matter of time.

He let her hand go, resting it carefully in the sand, then rose to his feet. "No sign of Andre?" he asked quietly.

"Last I saw him was when the raft overturned," Quinn said helplessly.

"Yeah," Herm added.

Dallas looked to Harper but she was crying into her hands. "You sure she's okay?" he asked.

"No I'm not fucking *okay!*" she screamed, her head snapping up, blue eyes wild. "This is fucking bullshit! Why haven't they found us already? I want to go home!"

The others stood there, unsure of what to do or say.

As if on cue, Gino Cortese emerged from a nearby section of jungle looking like a rugged outdoorsman straight out of central casting. His skin, tanned a deep brown, was the least damaged by the sun of them all, and in a tank top, shorts and sneakers, his sculpted body looked even more impressive than usual. Gino was strong, agile and confident, and looked it. His short dark hair was mussed, and but for a few scrapes and blisters, he seemed none the worse for wear. He made his way to Dallas and the two old friends embraced. It was a quick hug, and then Gino realized what he was doing and took a quick step back. "Good to see you, bro," he mumbled.

"He thought you were dead," Herm said suddenly.

Gino glared at him.

"That *is* what you said, isn't it? Dallas and Andre are gone and we need to face that and worry about those of us who are still alive, right?"

"Herm," Quinn sighed. "Jesus."

"What were you doing in the jungle?" Dallas asked, hoping to distract him.

Gino returned his attention to Dallas. "Little recon. Trying to figure out what we're dealing with here. I'm gonna need to get up high and check things out, but I think this is a relatively small island. Uninhabited, of course, but we need to assess the situation as best we can as quickly as we can."

"It's 2014," Herm said, brushing sand from his jeans. "It's only a matter of time before they find us. Come on, bunch of Americans lost at sea on vacation? I'm sure we're all over the news back home and I bet they've had all kinds of planes and ships out looking for us ever since that first night. They'll find us."

"You've been saying that for days," Quinn reminded him.

"The question is *where* are they looking?" Gino said.

"On the moon," Herm chuckled, "where do you think?"

It struck Dallas as obscene that, given the circumstances, Herm could laugh about anything, even cynically.

"Listen, genius," Gino said, "when the boat went down Murdoch said he got a mayday out. Meaning they knew where we *were*. That storm lasted all night, you can be sure it carried us pretty far from there. Then we drifted in the raft for three days after that. No telling how far from the original site we were by the time the second storm hit and blew us even farther away. We could be hundreds of miles from where the yacht went down. I'm sure they're looking for us too. Problem is they're probably just not looking anywhere around here."

"That's encouraging," Quinn mumbled.

"It's the truth," Gino said. "And it's important that we deal with the truth at this point, and to not lie to ourselves or deal in anything but the reality of what we're faced with here."

"One reality," Dallas said, "is I need water."

"Luckily, that we have."

"We do?"

Gino cocked his head toward the palm trees. "Come on."

Dallas followed him across the sand to what he soon realized was a piece of the raft that had been stretched out and secured with vines to two sticks sunk deep into the sand. Nearly three inches of water floated there, cupped by the makeshift rubber tray.

"Only good thing about the storm last night was it brought rain," Gino said. "I rigged that up fast as I could so we could at least catch some of it. Gonna have to put together something better soon as we can, but for now, it beats nothing."

Dallas dropped to his knees, greedily scooped up two handfuls of water and drank them down. His lips and throat felt better almost immediately, and the water, though warm, was the best thing he'd ever tasted.

"Easy, it's not the most secure set up," Gino told him. "And don't take too much, that's all we've got. Who knows when it'll rain again?"

"Sorry," he gasped, wiping what remained on his lips and chin into his mouth.

"Don't be sorry. We just need to be smart."

Dallas nodded. "Never been so thirsty," he said softly. He'd been wondering how everyone had the strength they'd exhibited. Now he knew. Once again, Gino had come through.

On the raft, there was bottled water Gino had as part of an emergency kit he'd brought with him on the boat, but Dallas hadn't had anything to drink since. At the time, everyone made fun of Gino's paranoia, chalking it up as his typical over-the-top survivalist nonsense. But when things went bad, had it not been for that canvas bag of bottled water and energy bars he'd insisted on bringing along, they may not have survived those three days adrift.

Together, Dallas and Gino returned to the others. Quinn was kneeling next to Natalie, holding her hand, head bowed and chapped lips moving slowly in prayer. Harper had wandered down by to the water's edge and was gazing out at the ocean, and Herm stood watching her, absently scratching at his crotch.

"Hey, perv," Gino said.

Herm grinned at him.

"Thought I told you to go get the raft?"

"Yeah, you did."

"Then go get it before it washes back out. We can use it, and that paddle too."

Herm looked to Dallas as if for help. "Okay, when did we all elect Gino commandant? Did I miss that meeting?"

"Just do it, asshole." Gino stepped toward him. "We need to work together, understand?"

"That's your idea of working together? *Just do it, asshole?* Seriously?" Herm shook his head. "You know I haven't had a cigarette in four days. I'm about ready to kill somebody as it is, so maybe you should take your Daniel Boone horseshit and stick it right up your ass, how's that sound?"

Before Gino could react Dallas stepped between them, took Herm by the shoulder and led him away. "Look, I know everyone's on edge, okay? We're all traumatized and exhausted and hungry and thirsty, but Gino's right, we need to—"

"He can go fuck himself. He talks to me like I'm a piece of shit, Dal."

"I know, I know. He doesn't mean it like that. It's just Gino's way. He's not exactly the most diplomatic person, you know? Deep down, he's not a bad guy, and we need him, Herm. You understand? We *need* him. He's forgotten more about staying alive in a place like this than we'll ever know. Just do what he says, okay? He'll keep us alive, but you got to trust him."

"And put up with his bullshit?"

"Yes, and put up with his bullshit."

Herm held his stare a while, then gave a slow nod and sighed heavily. "Okay."

"Go get what's left of the raft."

Dallas turned and walked back across the sand to the others. Gino had apparently already moved on to other things, as he was assessing a large rock-faced cliff at the far end of the island.

"There," he said, pointing. "I need to get up there."

"I don't think that's going to be too easy."

"It'll be okay."

"You need to be careful, Gino. Something happens to you, we're screwed."

"We're already screwed, partner."

"I mean it. We need you. We won't make it without you."

"Yeah, well some of us probably won't make it anyway." He looked past him to Herm, who was quite a distance away now. "Andre was strong and in shape, smart and a good swimmer. He doesn't make it, and that bag of shit does. Unbelievable."

"Herm's just—"

"He's weak."

Dallas looked into Gino's dark eyes, and for the first time saw something he'd never noticed before. There was coldness there, one of pure instinct guided by a primal need to survive. He'd always been guarded emotionally, and was often hardcore and a very no-nonsense, cut-and-dry sort of guy, but this was something much greater than that. Deeper...deadlier...

"Guess there's a slight chance Andre could still be alive out there somewhere," Gino said. "Or maybe even on some other part of the island. Unlikely, though."

Although Gino and Andre had been closer, Dallas had known Andre for years as well, and it seemed impossible he could really be gone. Even now, when Dallas thought of him he saw Andre with that big bright smile and contagious laugh, a tall and good-looking guy over six feet and with a sculpted body from years in the gym. It did seem strange that he'd been lost while someone of Herm's limited physical capabilities had survived. But nature was not only brutal; it could also be arbitrary.

"Can't believe he's really gone," Dallas managed, "doesn't seem possible."

"None of this shit does, but it is. Sooner we get our heads around it the better."

"Does Nat know?"

"She doesn't know anything. She's been out of it since I dragged her out of the surf." He drew a deep breath, let it out slowly. "She'll die without having to know about him, so there's that at least."

Just days before they'd all been so happy and carefree, on vacation, so certain their lives were playing out just as they should, and that nothing could go wrong…and now this…

"Gonna need to set some things straight," Gino said evenly. "Once asshole gets back with the raft, I'm gonna talk to everyone at once so we're all on the same page and know what we need to do from here. Need you to have my back on this, got it?"

"Yeah," Dallas said with a nod, "of course."

Gino gave him a quick playful punch to the shoulder, his way of saying thanks.

"I need to ask you," Dallas said, lowering his voice. "What are our chances, man? I mean, I know they're not good, but, really, what are they?"

"You want odds?"

"Just the truth."

"You already know the truth." Gino's dark eyes shifted to the ocean. "My guess is they'll search an area of tens of thousands of miles, but it's hard to know for sure. If we're hundreds of miles south of the Cook Islands like I think we are, the odds of them finding us are almost zero, though. We may never leave here, not alive, anyway."

"You really believe that?"

"None of us can afford to believe that. But unless we get miracle-level lucky, odds are we're gonna be on this island for a long time."

The white sand, the palm trees and jungle, the enormous blue sky and clear water, it all should've been so beautiful—and it was—but it was something else too, something dangerous and deadly, something imprisoning them, holding them hostage from the rest of the world and everyone else in it. In that moment, Dallas thought about home for the first time since those endless hours in the raft, when there was nothing to do but pray for rescue, reflect on your life and wonder if that was where it would all end, floating aimlessly in that horrible little rubber raft.

"Come on," Gino said, bringing him back.

As they returned to the others, Herm appeared, meandering awkwardly across the sand and dragging the remains of the raft behind him. Once closer, he dropped it then began pointing and motioning to it with both hands, like a spokesmodel.

"Okay, Tonto?" he said to Gino.

"All right everyone," he said, ignoring him, "listen up."

Harper, who had been down by the water, wandered back, eyes red from crying. Quinn remained with Nat, holding her hands, but looked over at them, and Herm dropped down to the sand with a weary grunt.

"Okay, so here's the deal," Gino said, hesitating a moment before continuing. "The fact of the matter is we don't have any idea when we'll get out of here. Until then, we need to take certain steps to make sure we have the best chance for survival. This isn't a resort, and we're not on vacation anymore."

Herm shook his head and looked to Dallas. "Is this guy serious?"

"Herm, please," Dallas said. "Be quiet and listen to the man."

"We're not on vacation anymore? Really, I mean, who knew?"

"You gonna listen or run your mouth?" Gino asked.

"We just spent three days in a goddamn raft in the middle of the Pacific Ocean. We lost Andre, Nat and Murdoch are both badly hurt and the rest of us have been through hell, I'm relatively certain we're all well aware we're not on *fucking* vacation anymore. But by all means, continue, and please, be even more condescending if at all possible."

"You think this is a game? You think this is a joke? If we don't do things right from here on out, we'll die, you understand? We'll die."

"At least we're on solid ground again, Donna Drama. I'd say things are looking up. We had a hell of lot less chance out there in the open ocean."

Gino put hands on his hips and looked away, collecting himself. "I don't have to do any of this. I know how to survive here, got it? I'm trying to help you. If we work together we might—*might*—be all right. But we have to stick together, work smart, and know what to do and what not to do. You want to fend for yourself, Herm? You got this all figured out? Feel free, I don't give a shit. But everybody else wants and needs to hear what I have to say, and we don't have lots of time to be standing around talking, we need to get to work. You're making that harder, and I'm not gonna allow you to jeopardize our lives with your wiseass bullshit."

"Can you even hear yourself over that ridiculous ego? You won't *allow* it?"

"No, motherfucker, I won't." Gino squared his stance, arms down at his sides but hands clenched into fists. "So listen to me very carefully. Sit there and shut-up, or fuck off. You're on my last fucking nerve. And that's nowhere you want to be, chief."

Herm gave a mock shiver. "*Please*, you're frightening me."

"Can't you just be quiet?" Quinn asked. "Even for just a little while?"

Dallas caught Herm's gaze and slowly shook his head in warning. Gino was not someone he wanted to get physical with, and they all knew it. Subtly, he moved a bit closer, just in case he had to try to stop him from beating Herm senseless.

When it became apparent no one was going to side with or even defend him, Herm went from smirking to holding his hands up like the victim of a robbery. "All right," he finally said. "Fine, go ahead."

"Water, food, shelter," Gino said. "We need all three. Water we have for now, though it's limited. We can put together better rain catchers and a system so that when it rains we'll be able to collect as much as possible. Problem is we have no idea how often or for how long it'll rain. The second option is to boil saltwater and even build a solar still to convert our urine to drinkable water, if it comes to that. On saltwater, it's more complicated, but I'm confident I can rig a workable system, depending on what I can piece together. Like I told you guys on the raft, water is essential. Most people can last a few weeks without food. It sucks and you'll be sick as hell, but you can survive. Without water, we'll all be dead in three or four days. As for food, that isn't as much of an issue. The island isn't large enough to support any kind of animal population for us to eat, I don't think, maybe rodents or select insects, possibly even some reptilian life, but it's hard to know yet. Same with the vegetation, in that there's likely some of it that's edible but I have to take a closer look around the island. Honestly, I'm not as educated in that area as I should be, but I can likely identify some flora here we can eat. The good news is there's an ocean all around us, and it's full of food. The bad news is we have to catch or find it. But again, I can rig fishing apparatus and probably even some traps once I find the right materials. Also, there's an abundance of coconuts from the palm trees, many already all over the ground. They're essential for our survival, because they can provide us with a decent food source, but liquid nourishment too. Thing is, it's not like in the movies, though, the fuckers are hard as hell and really difficult to open without a lot of force or a decent tool, something super sharp. I can fashion tools from rocks, hopefully something that'll help us split the coconuts without too much trouble, but these things don't just appear, I'll need to make them, and I'll need your help. Everyone's got to do their part, understand?

"Finally," he continued, "shelter. I think we can all agree that after last night, being out on this beach isn't gonna work for long. We're too out in the open and too exposed to the elements. Now this could be trickier. I noticed some rock formations a ways down the shoreline. There could be caves there, and they might work, we'll have to investigate that. Otherwise, we can build basic lean-tos that'll be enough to protect us from the elements. It's going to take a lot of hard work on all of our parts, and that's where the water becomes so vital. These things are going to take time and they're going to be a challenge, don't misunderstand me. But without enough water, especially in this heat, we won't have the strength or means to get any of this done. So that's priority number one. We start by making some hard decisions. It's the way things have to be. It's about survival now, and we all have to understand that, because even if we do everything right, even if we get all the breaks, we can still die out here very easily."

"Tell us what to do and we'll do it," Dallas said.

"We have to be careful with what little water we have." Gino frowned, looked to Quinn. "I know you've been giving Nat some now and then."

Quinn nodded. "Just a little," she said softly.

"No more."

Quinn looked incredulous. "I just wet her lips and give her tiny sips when she's conscious, Gino, that's all."

"That's too much."

"Then I'll give her some out of my ration, okay?"

"No, it's not okay, because we need you strong and you need

that water to be strong. We'll all be functioning on less water than we'll need to begin with. We need to do certain things to survive. They may not all be pretty or seem fair, some will seem anything but. They'll be brutal and hardcore, but they're necessary. Bottom line, Nat's not gonna get any better, Quinn. We all know this. That water's precious. We can't waste any of it on her."

"He's right," Murdoch said suddenly.

Until then, no one had thought he was conscious.

"And if I don't get any better, I'm useless to you," he added. "So don't give me any either."

Quinn left Natalie and went to him, taking his hands. "Easy," she said. "It's going to be all right."

"Yeah," he muttered, "okay, kid."

"No question we have to make some tough choices," Dallas said. "But we need to do that without losing our humanity. We're still—I mean, for God's sake—we still—"

"He's unconscious again." Quinn gently placed Murdoch's arms over his chest then crawled back over to Natalie.

"Another thing," Gino said. "I don't want any of you going anywhere on your own, understand? An island like this can be a very dangerous place. Wandering off on your own could be lethal."

"What about fire?" Herm asked. "Even I know we need fire."

"Yeah," Harper said, finally speaking with her little-girl-like voice they'd all once found comical. "Last night was the darkest night

I've ever seen, it was really scary."

Herm rolled his eyes. "Well, there you have it."

"That's why those eyeglasses you're wearing are gonna come in handy," Gino said. "But before we do anything else, we need to agree on the water. We ration it, but only between us and—"

"Doesn't matter," Quinn said.

"Quinn, look, I don't like it any more than you do, but—"

"I said it doesn't matter. Nat won't be drinking anymore of our water." As the others looked to her, she stood, shaking, tears streaming her face. "She just died."

CHAPTER TWO

Later, the nightmares faded, and Quinn would dream of Natalie and Andre, of her life back home with Dallas and the others she knew and loved. She would see them in her dreams, watching her, sometimes even comforting her, telling her they were all right, that they missed her and would one day see her again. The horrors of the stormy night the boat sank haunted her for days, her memories of plunging into darkness, being swallowed by the ocean and struggling to the surface only to find a violent and surging sea that tossed her about like a ragdoll, those moments remained with her, and always would. The chaos and horror, aimlessly floating in the raft, slowly dying beneath a merciless sun while sharks circled, waiting on them, those outside the raft struggling to get as much of themselves up and out of the water as they could without tipping the whole thing over, and a primal terror unlike anything she or the others had ever known, all those things had become part of her now. Sometimes they'd creep about at the outskirts of her dreams, as if to remind her they hadn't gone so very far after all, but then light would come, and Quinn would be so sure it was rescue, only to understand seconds later it was instead the sun of a new day, another day. There, on the island, in a place as hopeless, unforgiving and brutal as it was beautiful. And in those quiet, lonely and agonizing moments, Quinn was certain none of them would ever leave this place. Even in death, she and the others would be trapped here. Forever...

In those first days on the island, they did their best to build some semblance of a camp on the beach, and followed Gino's instructions on how to get things done. While he made his living in a corporate setting, wearing a suit and tie and sitting at a desk, Gino was an adrenaline junkie and survival enthusiast that had spent years of his free time studying survival techniques and challenging himself by applying them all over the world on numerous vacations that involved everything from deep woods adventures in the Pacific Northwest to survivalist expeditions in Australia's Outback, the wilds of Alaska, Africa's Serengeti, the jungles of South America and beyond. He was a skilled tracker and hunter, an avid rock climber, a whitewater rafting, skydiving and scuba enthusiast, and possessed a wide array of adventure expertise. Gino also knew quite a bit about plant and animal life, as well as how to survive in various terrains and under a wide assortment of conditions. For the rest, a vacation to a resort on the Cook Islands involving swimming and sunning and a fishing trip aboard a sporting yacht was quite an adventure, but for Gino it had been one of his tamer excursions.

Until it all went wrong, and suddenly, he was back in his element.

Water was not an immediate concern, so Gino had them set

about obtaining what they needed for food and shelter. After he'd shown them which kinds to take from the edges of the jungle, Herm and Dallas gathered leaves and branches for use in building a quick shelter, while Harper collected some of the coconuts that had fallen to the ground, separating out those that had already begun to rot. Meanwhile, Gino scoured the rocky section of coastline along the island until he'd located stones he could utilize, and by chipping them against other rocks, had fashioned a couple into makeshift but effective tools that were capable of cutting flora, and with a great deal of effort and patience, cracking the outer shell of coconuts enough to begin and make easier the process of splitting them.

The heat was a problem, and the harder they worked the more water they needed, so Gino insisted they work slowly but efficiently, taking frequent breaks and sipping water only when they absolutely could not continue without it.

After digging a small pit and surrounding it with stones, he and Dallas found the items necessary to get a fire going. Using the lens on Herm's eyeglasses, after numerous tries and angles, Gino managed to produce smoke, and eventually a flame he was able to sustain and expertly nurse into a full-fledged fire. Once it was strong enough, he left Herm in charge of keeping it going, then he and Dallas gathered the sturdiest sticks they could find, so that later, using the sharp-edged stones, they could whittle the ends into points and turn them into makeshift fishing spears.

When it could be put off no longer, Gino and Dallas buried Natalie.

Quinn had known Gino almost as long as Dallas had, and though he and her husband were much closer friends, she liked Gino, albeit in small doses. He grated on her as well, as he could be maddeningly boorish, pompous, condescending and a highly opinionated know-it-all. Never married, he ran around with women considerably younger than he was, usually the type that was no threat or challenge to him intellectually, and that possessed a particular vacuous look and body type. He was the shallow male chauvinist type Quinn usually abhorred, but Gino could also be quite charming when he wanted to be, thoughtful and kind, the type of person who would stop everything he was doing to help his friends. Though usually intense and brooding, he could also be funny and a lot of fun when the mood struck him. But he was, as Dallas often described him, an acquired taste. In this situation however, Quinn was grateful he was with them. Without him, she and the others would likely no longer still be alive.

Through the glaring sun, she watched as Gino and Dallas pushed the final handfuls of dirt and sand over the hole they'd dug and in which they'd placed Natalie's nude body. Despite Quinn's objections, Gino had insisted they strip her, because her clothing could be used. Between the two rows of palm trees farther down the beach, they'd buried her as best they could. Quinn still couldn't believe Nat was gone, that she died right there in front of her. Just hours before, in the raft, it had been Natalie who had assured them all that everything would be all right and that one day they'd look back on this as the adventure it had been. She'd always been optimistic, even back in the world. It didn't seem fair.

Quinn had once been an EMT. She'd seen her share of carnage and even death, and that was what had ultimately led her to leave the profession and return to school to get her business degree. She'd worked as an area manager for a retail clothing store ever since. Quinn had never quit anything in her life until then. At first the adrenaline rush and the ability to help, and in some cases even save the lives of others, had kept her going. But when a call led her to a car accident where two children were among the bloody victims killed, it changed something in her. It was too much. The faces of those children haunted her, and she'd gone to a psychologist to help her deal with it. Nothing had ever affected her like that before or since, until now, until these last few days of madness. Watching one of her best friends die in the sand as she held her hands was more personal and worse than the broken bodies of those dead children. Natalie should've been spared, Quinn thought, just like those innocent children. Natalie was the one who'd always looked out for them, for everyone, always put herself last.

"You okay?"

She turned and saw Herm a few feet behind her, his arms full of small sticks, leaves and other light burnable vegetation he'd found at the edge of the jungle and gathered as Gino had instructed.

"Quinn," he said when she didn't answer, "you all right?"

"I don't know," she said with a shrug. "This is a nightmare."

"Yeah," he said softly. "If only we could wake up, huh?"

She wiped another wave of tears from her eyes and nodded.

"I'm sorry," he said. "I know you two were close. I didn't know Nat as well as you guys, but she was a good person. Over the last few days, I...I felt like I got to know her better and—I—anyway—I'm sorry."

Quinn managed a slight smile. "Thanks, Herm." She motioned to the sticks and things in his arms. "Need some help?"

"No, you better not. I have to wait for further instructions from the supreme commander." He chuckled. "But Shipwreck Barbie could probably use a hand."

Quinn followed his gaze in the direction opposite Natalie's grave, where Harper was gathering and piling coconuts that had fallen from the trees forty yards or so in the distance. She'd already formed one small pile and continued listlessly moving back and forth, bending and picking up coconuts then bringing them to the pile and dropping them amongst the others.

"I know we're all scared," Quinn said, "but that poor thing is terrified."

"Of course she is. What is she, fourteen?"

"Twenty-three, actually."

"Imagine a guy like Gino dating a twenty-something beach bunny bimbo twelve years younger than he is. What a shocker."

"Hey, you've been checking her out and you're old enough to be her father."

"I'm not dating her though, but thanks for reminding me."

The fact was Herm wasn't dating anyone. In all the years she'd known him he'd only had one girlfriend and that hadn't lasted more than a few months. "I don't think she's a bad person," Quinn said, "just a little limited, that's all."

"Also doesn't help that she sounds like Smurfette."

"You're terrible." Quinn forced a weary smile.

"True, but at least I got a smile out of you." Herm basked in that a moment. "What do you suppose they talk about? It's got to be hysterical, right? I mean no matter what it is."

Unable to prevent another smile, Quinn shook her head and headed off in Harper's direction. "I'm going to go see if I can help."

"You're right, probably best not to encourage me."

Quinn trudged away across the hot sand in her bare feet. She'd always felt sorry for Herm, as she knew Dallas did. He was a bit of a sad case, and could often be an insufferable jerk, but he could also be extremely sweet, and had an uncanny ability to find humor in even the worst circumstances. As fear-based, cutting and inappropriate as that humor could sometimes be, there was still value in it, Quinn thought. She'd just lost her friend, and although they hadn't found Andre and likely never would, they'd lost him too. Yet he'd made her smile. No small task, she thought, glancing back over her shoulder.

Herm stood there holding his sticks and watching her like

the lost soul he was. He'd never looked quite so alone, and there was something disturbing about that, as if he'd realized it just then too. But neither of them could do anything about it. Neither of them could do anything about any of this.

As Quinn got closer to the trees, Harper noticed her.

Dropping a coconut to the sand, Harper inspected her hand with a look of disgust. "Broke a nail," she said, rolling her eyes. "Only got a couple left."

"Looks like you're making out all right otherwise."

Harper pointed to the coconuts she'd gathered. "Is this enough, or, like…"

"Yeah, I'd say so."

"Good, because they're, like, really gross. I don't even like coconuts."

"Come on," Quinn said, bending down, "let's carry these back."

Wringing her hands, Harper looked down at the sand. "Quinn, can I ask you something?"

"Sure."

"Are we going to die here?" She bit her bottom lip, and began to cry.

Quinn reached out and touched her arm. She knew the real answer was she had no idea, but instead said, "Of course not. Don't cry."

"You think we'll get rescued?" She sniffled.

"Maybe not right away but…yeah, sure I do."

"Really?"

"I know it's hard, but you have to try to hold it together, okay? We all do."

"I've been too busy falling apart." Harper laughed nervously then grew quiet and serious. "I'm sorry about Nat. I didn't know her that good, but she was a nice person."

"Yes, she was."

"I never saw anybody die before. I never even knew anybody that died, except for my great grandma. She died when I was little but she was mad old." Harper shook her head, as if doing so might better illustrate her point. "I'm a server at JUGGIES, what do I know about death anyways? If you want yummy appetizers or a drink from the bar, I got you, right? But I—I can't believe this is happening. It's like a movie. I just want to go home, you know? I want to, like, take a shower and get in my jammies and play with my kitty— I miss her *so* bad—for real. I want my iPhone so I can talk to my friends and post and chat and hang out, and I want to have drinks and dance and have fun, I—I don't want… *this*. This sucks."

Quinn nodded, unsure of how to respond to any of that.

"Gino gets mad at me sometimes because I don't pay attention to all that survival stuff he's into. But, like, that's just not me. I'm more into fun stuff. YOLO, girl. Right? I may not know a lot of things, but we should've never gone on that stupid boat. We could've just stayed on the beach or at the hotel and stuff, it was so beautiful there. It's beautiful here too but it scares me. Does it scare you too?"

"A little bit, yes."

Harper offered a cartoonish frown. "Can I ask you something else, Quinn?"

For the love of God, I wish you wouldn't. "Okay."

"Do you think Andre's all right?"

"I guess there's no way to know for sure, but no, Harper, I don't."

She grimaced, and more tears came.

"Come on," Quinn said softly, crouching down again. "I'll help you with these."

Harper wiped her tears. "Quinn?"

"Yeah?" she said through a heavy sigh.

"Thanks for being so nice."

Though it took some effort, Quinn smiled then began gathering the coconuts.

Suddenly, she looked out into the jungle. A strong sensation that someone was watching them flooded through her with such ferocity, it caused a chill to dance along the back of her neck even in the relentless heat.

"What's wrong?" Harper asked, wide-eyed.

Rather than answer, Quinn stared into the jungle, slowly scanning it back and forth, looking for anything out of the ordinary. Nothing…yet she couldn't shake the feeling they were being watched by someone…or something…and either way, it wasn't friendly. A primal sense of danger took hold of her, and her instinctual reaction was to run. But she held her ground.

"Why are you doing that?" Harper persisted. "You're scaring me."

A warm wind blew in off the ocean, rustling the edge of the jungle as it passed through, like a whisper. And then, quickly as it arrived, the feeling was gone, as if it had escaped on the breeze.

"Nothing," Quinn said absently, her body gradually relaxing. "I thought…"

"What?"

"It's nothing. It's okay."

Quinn returned to gathering coconuts, and thankfully Harper joined her without further questions or monologues, and together, they carried several back to the others.

As they walked the beach, her arms full, Quinn looked back twice. But there was nothing, no one, only jungle, sand and a glaring sun.

Having finished the burial, Dallas walked across the sand to the water and slowly waded in. Gino went right to work, telling Quinn and Harper they'd done well then taking Herm with him up closer to the tree line to stoke the fire.

Quinn watched Dallas in the water. She knew him better than anyone, and understood it was more than the dirt he was attempting to cleanse himself of. Emotion got the better of her, and she steeled herself, looking away and back down the stretch of beach from which she'd come.

"So, like, now what?" Harper asked, dropping the coconuts to the ground.

Murdoch still lying a few feet away, groaned, as if on cue.

"Why don't you sit with him for a while?" Quinn suggested.

Harper scrunched her face up and leaned in close, lowering her voice. "He kind of freaks me out, with, you know, his eyes like that and stuff."

"John?" Quinn asked. "Are you awake?"

He turned his head, following the sound of her voice, his eyes caked and closed, covered with dried blood. She'd dabbed at them and cleaned them earlier as best she could, but due to the severity of the gashes hadn't been able to attend to them as sufficiently as she'd have liked. In addition to the excruciating pain he was surely feeling, infection was the main enemy, and with no access to antibiotics or even anything to properly dress the wounds, she knew that even if they were meticulously careful with him, it was highly probable one would eventually set in anyway. So keeping him comfortable and even somewhat hydrated was paramount.

"Quinn?" he asked.

"Yes," she said. "I'm here. Can you walk?"

"I think maybe, yeah."

Quinn turned to Harper. "Help him up and get him over there to the trees so he can have some shade and shelter. We can't just leave him here out in the open under this hot sun."

"*Me?*" Harper mouthed silently. "*Can't you?*"

"Harper's going to help you, John," she said. "She's going to get you into some shade, all right?"

"Okay, yeah that—that's good."

Harper put her hands on her hips and cocked her head in what Quinn could only assume was supposed to be a look of annoyance. "Chica, seriously?"

"Yeah," Quinn said evenly, "seriously."

Without another word, Quinn walked away. She couldn't take another second of this airhead, and was afraid if she didn't get some physical separation she was going to tell her so. More conflict was the last thing everyone needed, so she did her best to summon the tools she'd acquired as an EMT, when she'd often have to not only care for those injured, but diffuse a situation before, during and sometimes even after doing so.

She breathed deeply, walked along the sand and tried to clear her mind. Her legs were still weak and a bit shaky from having not been used or bearing any weight for three days in the raft, but they were slowly regaining their strength. Her stomach grumbled from hunger, and the nearly constant thirst she'd endured for days was back.

It all still seemed like a dream. A horrible dream, but a dream nonetheless. These things didn't happen to everyday people. Yet here they were.

The more she thought about it, the more she understood Gino's harshness and cold, calculating approach to things. He was right. They'd never survive without taking certain measures.

She looked back down the beach, saw Harper playing with her hair and gazing up at the sun. Her lips were moving so she was obviously talking to Murdoch.

Natalie's face flashed across her mind's eye, and Quinn found herself crying quietly as she walked along the water's edge. *Get yourself together*, she thought, hearing Natalie's voice in her head instead of her own. *You have to be strong now.*

Quinn wiped her eyes, and that's when she saw it.

A shoe, lying in the wet sand just beyond the reach of the water, a sneaker she recognized. For a second, she froze, staring at it and trying to convince herself it was actually there. Looking back at the jungle, Quinn realized this was almost exactly where she'd had the feeling of being watched. She took a step closer to the sneaker. It was on its side but pointed in the direction of the jungle, as if the person wearing it had stepped out of it just a few feet onto the beach, then continued on without it. Had it been last night, she thought, if one lost a shoe, one would likely never be able to locate it in such unfathomable darkness. Quinn crouched down and picked it up.

Like an electrical current, a surge of emotions coursed through her. Andre.

The sneaker was Andre's.

Chapter Three

Dallas hated the ocean. He'd grown to despise it in these last few days. No longer was it a beautiful and majestic entity of wonder and awe, but instead a heartless monstrosity teeming with predators and dangers that existed for no reason other than to destroy him and those he loved. Were it up to him, despite having grown up an avid swimmer and beachgoer and having lived within walking distance of the Atlantic Ocean for the majority of his life, were he to never lay eyes on an ocean again it would be too soon. But in this case, with grit and sand and remnants of Natalie—her perspiration and even her smell—on his skin, he had no choice but to walk out into the waves and let them cleanse him as nothing else here could. Although Gino apparently felt no need to do the same, and had instead gone about his duties, Dallas ventured out until the water was up to his chest. The tide was strong and his legs were still weak, but he was able to remain upright. After a few moments, he let his body fall back so that he was partially floating, though he could still feel the bottom with his toes. As the back of his head touched the water, he looked up into the deadly sun and closed his eyes, letting the sway of the waves rock him slowly back and forth. He tried to force the visions of Natalie's dead, limp body from his mind, focusing instead on the pain in his chest. It still hurt a bit when he took a deep breath, but he was relatively certain it was getting better. He couldn't be sure if something was hurt inside him or if it was just another symptom of stress and exhaustion. Either way, he had no plans to mention it to anyone, not even Quinn. There was no room for weakness here. Dallas understood that all too well now. Gino wasn't playing games. He'd known him since their college days, long enough to realize that regardless of what happened from here on out, Gino had every intention of surviving this ordeal. That much was painfully clear, and although Dallas outwardly showed concern and questioned his friend in the hopes he could keep him at least somewhat grounded in all this madness, secretly, he agreed with him. Whatever it took, he and Quinn were getting off this island. They were getting home, or he'd die in the attempt. Either way, much as his conscience wanted to condemn Gino, Dallas knew that were it to become necessary, he'd be no different in the final analysis. Could he be as brutal as Gino likely could be, though? If he were backed into a corner, could he come out swinging with such vengeance and desire to survive that it made no difference who or what had to get hurt in the process? It was about living or dying now, nothing more. Maybe it always had been. Andre was gone, probably dead. It was time to face that, to get his mind around it not only conceptually, but as a cold hard fact. Like the vision of poor Natalie, nude and dead, rolling lifelessly into that makeshift grave, looking as if she were asleep and might at any moment open her eyes, stand up and assure them it was all some elaborate bad joke. He clenched his eyes shut tighter, but the pictures in his mind refused to let him go. Natalie was dead and nothing was going to bring her back. A sweet and wonderful person who wouldn't hurt a fly was one of the first among them to go, along with Andre, who other than Gino, was the strongest and most physically fit of the group. What did that tell him? That all bets were off, and although it might not yet be necessary to behave as such, when the time came, he'd be ready to do whatever he had to do in order to make sure he and Quinn survived.

With a tangle of thoughts and fears coursing through him, it was the sound of Quinn's voice that brought him back. He sat up quickly, his hair dripping water as he spun back toward shore, his eyes panning across the waterline in search of his wife's voice. She was calling for everyone to come, and even before he'd managed to locate her through the glare, he was wading fast as he could toward shore.

By the time he'd made the sand, Gino was sprinting down the beach toward her, Herm and Harper walking well behind him and far less urgent in their movements.

Though his legs were not quite ready for the strain, Dallas pushed them anyway. Running with a bit of a hobble, and at nowhere near the speed he normally could have, he closed on Quinn, who had seen him too and was motioning for him, even though Gino was already at her side.

When he got within a few feet of them, he saw she was holding something.

"It's Andre's," Gino told him before she could.

Dallas, out of breath, wiped his eyes and took a closer look. "Yeah," he said. "It is. Where did you find it?"

"There." Quinn pointed to the section of sand where she'd first seen it. "It was just lying there."

Herm and Harper had joined them now.

"What does it mean?" Harper asked.

"Gonna roll the dice on this one," Herm said. "You ask that a lot, don't you?"

Harper cocked her head. "Huh?"

"Doesn't necessarily mean anything," Gino said, looking out at the ocean then back at the jungle, his eyes squinting. "He could've just lost his shoe in the surf and it cleared the reef but his body never did."

"But if his body was out there," Quinn said, "on this side of the reef, it would've washed ashore by now."

"Yeah, it would've."

"So he could still be alive?" Dallas asked hopefully.

"If he came ashore last night and lost his sneaker right there," Gino said, pointing, "it was so dark he could've made his way into the jungle and we would've never seen him."

"But isn't it safe to assume he would've seen us by now?" Herm asked.

"Not if he's hurt," Quinn said. "He could be lying just a few feet inside the jungle and we'd never know he was there."

As a group, they hurried across the sand to the jungle.

They cleared the two rows of palm trees then stopped, looking for the best route into the jungle. Although accessible, rather than gradual, the vegetation was sudden and thick in places, which made visibility difficult. There was no telling what awaited them beyond the edge of the jungle.

Quinn thought of mentioning the strange feeling she'd had earlier, but decided against it. The sensation, though strong at the time, was gone and had not returned.

"Everybody stay together," Gino said, pushing his way in, "and stay behind me. Single file, watch your step and keep your eyes open."

Things became immediately darker in the thickness of the jungle, which included a heavy canopy of vegetation and trees. Sunlight cut through in beams crisscrossing before them, and the heat remained a constant. Here, unseen things crawled and slithered and made strange sounds, reminding Gino and the others that they were the intruders, the aliens in this foreign world. Quinn had reluctantly taken Natalie's sandals, and although they were a little small, they were preferable to being barefoot, particularly once they'd left the sand, something Dallas quickly realized as the only member of the group still without shoes. Pulling up the rear, he glanced behind them every few seconds to make certain he knew the path they were following and where to go to find their way back out. Regardless of how deep they went, the jungle essentially looked the same, so becoming disoriented and lost within it was highly probable were one not careful.

The ground was uneven and treacherous, and Dallas soon lagged behind the others, as with each step the bottoms of his feet were subjected to progressively painful terrain. He'd have to come up with something, put together some sort of coverings or something for them, he thought, or his feet would never hold up and they'd soon be ravaged even worse with cuts and scrapes, which would not only leave him hobbled, but susceptible to infection. "Slow down, guys," he said, his body already drenched in sweat and his throat constricting and in need of water.

Quinn and Herm stopped and waited for him, but Gino and Harper continued on, pushing their way through the brush.

"No shoes," Dallas said. "I'm having trouble keeping up."

"How far are we supposed to go, anyway?" Herm asked.

"Why don't you go back to the beach and wait?" Quinn suggested.

"There's no sign of him anyway," Herm said, nodding in agreement. "And I may not be the survival expert Gino is, but I do know the more we exert ourselves in this heat the more water we're going to need. I don't have any desire to go on some wild goose chase looking for Andre when he may not even be here. His sneaker could've just washed ashore, for Christ's sake. It doesn't mean he made it to shore, and there's zero evidence he walked into the jungle."

"You guys head back," Quinn said, "I'll go with them and see if we can find anything."

Before Dallas could answer, a scream tore through the jungle from somewhere up ahead of them, a shriek so loud and horrific it sent several birds they hadn't even realized were there to erupt into flight.

Quinn parted the brush. Herm and Dallas followed her through and into a small natural clearing in the jungle. Harper had dropped to the ground and was weeping uncontrollably, her entire body shaking as Gino stood expressionless, staring at a thick and gnarled branch about three feet above the ground that protruded at a horizontal angle from the heavier brush surrounding it.

"Oh dear God," Quinn gasped.

When Dallas realized it wasn't the branch Gino was staring at, but rather what was on the ground beneath it, he saw it too. He knew it was real and right in front of him, but it simply wouldn't compute, his mind would not accept and process it. His stomach clenched, and it suddenly felt as if the bottom of the world had given way beneath his feet, sending him plummeting down into a dark chasm.

Harper's cries filled the silence.

"What the fuck?" Herm said breathlessly, pacing about awkwardly while wringing his hands. "What the *fuck*?"

Dallas felt his mouth go dry, and it was then he realized it was hanging open as he stared at a large rock a few feet ahead of him, and the severed human arm draped across it.

The left shoulder, arm and hand lay in a pool of blood and gristle, and chunks of flesh dangled from a knob of bone protruding from the shoulder, scraps of meat dried and discolored in the jungle heat.

CHAPTER FOUR

Dallas felt Quinn grab hold of him. Not to keep him upright, it turned out, but to keep herself from collapsing. Her body trembled, joining his, and they held each other close. In that impossibly surreal and terrifying moment, Harper continued to wail, Herm paced about like a caged animal and Gino stood silently staring at the carnage.

Finally, Harper got to her feet and ran back the way they came, mumbling something unintelligible and flailing her arms around like a madwoman.

After a moment, Herm went after her.

Dallas forced his eyes beyond his wife's shoulder and searched the surrounding area. "Gino," he heard himself say, his voice distant and weak before becoming more insistent. "Goddamn it, *Gino!*"

He turned to them.

Dallas had never seen him like this. His arrogance was gone, shattered. He was in shock like they were. "What the hell's—what—what is this, what—what happened?"

"I don't..." Gino blinked, shook his head. "I don't know."

Suddenly Dallas found himself looking at the lifeless hand, and a band on the ring finger he recognized as Andre's. "Jesus, that's really his fucking arm."

As Quinn let him go, Dallas brought a hand to his mouth, but it was too late. He spun away, doubled over and vomited, retching violently and expelling bile, as he had no food in his stomach.

Quinn kept a hand on her husband's back, but her attention was on Gino. "What could do that to him?" she asked.

"I-I don't know," Gino stammered. "I—an animal maybe—I don't know."

Hesitantly, she moved closer to the rock and looked at the arm, which was swarming with light-colored ants. Though her eyes had filled with tears, Quinn fell back on her training and wrestled her emotions into submission as best she could. She was still having trouble thinking clearly, and her body wouldn't stop shaking, but she kept pushing for control, and slowly, gradually, it began to return to her. "What kind of an animal would do that?"

"It'd have to be pretty big." Gino's face glistened with sweat. "And I don't see how an island this small, with a limited food supply, could support a species that size, especially a carnivore. It doesn't really add up, it..."

"What about a shark? He could've been attacked before he reached shore."

"It's possible, but it stands to reason it was more likely the reef."

"He's right," Quinn said. "A shark attack is possible. He could've been bitten, had his arm nearly taken off. Or he could've torn it up on the reef, made it to shore with his arm barely intact, then disoriented, in shock and lost in the dark, he ran across the sand and into the jungle. And then once he got to this point, with it already badly injured, he lost his arm."

Gino nodded. "Yeah, that...that could be, and it makes more sense."

"Where the hell..." Dallas wiped his mouth but two more waves of dry heaves throttled him before he could speak again. "Where the hell's the rest of him?"

"Andre!" Quinn called into the jungle before them. "Andre!"

"Stop," Gino said. "Quinn, *stop*, just...stop. Whatever happened, he would've lost so much blood that even if he'd somehow managed to stay conscious and was working on pure adrenaline, he would've been in a deep state of confusion and shock. He could've staggered off deeper into the jungle and collapsed somewhere nearby, but with that amount of blood loss there's no way he could still be alive."

Quinn knew he was right. Not only her training backed it up, but so did common sense. She stared at him helplessly. "Yeah, you—you're right."

He ran his hands through his hair and across his head, leaving them there as if fearful whatever else he was thinking might spill free otherwise. "I don't want to be right," Gino muttered. "Not this time. But we all know I am."

Look at it, Quinn told herself, summoning her training and as much courage as she could find. *Calm down, focus, and make an assessment.* She tried to see only a *thing* resting there on the rock, not a limb that had once been attached to a human being, and certainly not someone she'd known and cared about.

"Careful," Gino warned. "If those ants are what I think they are you don't want them on you."

She looked at him questioningly. "Do they bite?"

"I think they might be Yellow Crazies. They're found on some South Pacific islands. They don't bite. They spray acid."

"Of course they do," she said, wiping sweat from her brow with a heavy sigh.

"Just don't touch it."

Quinn had no intention of touching the limb, but that bit of news only served to make their nightmare even more horrific and surreal. Covering her nose against the smell, she leaned in for a closer look. It was impossible to know for sure, but a closer inspection revealed that despite the grisly look of it, and the bevy of ants all over it, the arm did not appear to be badly torn, as one would expect from the bite or ripping motion of a predator. "It's hard to tell," she said, "but it looks relatively clean. Almost like it was *cut*."

"In a way the reef could've?" Dallas asked.

"I don't know. It definitely doesn't look like a bite."

"Jesus," Dallas said through a sigh. "Are you saying somebody cut his arm off?"

"Of course not, I…"

"What then?"

Quinn moved away and looked out across the jungle, as if for answers. "I don't know, all right? I'm not a coroner. I'm just saying that to me it doesn't look like any kind of bite I've ever seen. I'm thinking it had to be the reef. It had to be."

"I can see how it could happen if he hit just right and got snagged on it," Dallas said. "But at the same time, would it be that clean?"

"If it's not that then—I mean, Dal—come on."

Gino finally dropped his hands but he still had no idea what to do with them. "Okay, let's just get one thing straight here. The odds that there's anyone else on this island are practically nonexistent."

"Why?" Dallas asked. "We're here, why couldn't someone else be?"

"Because we're in the middle of fucking nowhere."

"You'll have to do better than that."

"It's a million-to-one that *we* wound up here, much less anyone else. There aren't any native peoples who'd be out this far on some uncharted little useless stretch of land like this."

"How would you know?"

"Common sense, you've heard of that, right?"

"Honey," Quinn said, "I didn't say for sure it was cut, I said it looked like it might have been. The reef being responsible is a much more realistic—"

"Then where's the rest of him?" Dallas said. "We need to find him."

Gino motioned to the blood covering the nearby leaves and ground, and the wide swaths of it around the base of the rock. "We need to keep looking."

Quinn nodded and hugged herself. "He can't be far."

"But we're not sure what did this to him," Dallas said.

"It had to be the reef," Quinn answered. "How could there be anyone else here? Gino's right, the odds of us ending up here are astronomical. We could very well be the only people to ever set foot here, and even if we aren't, it's likely we're the first in a very long time."

Dallas thought a moment, trying desperately to quiet the storm in his head. Quinn was likely right, but something deep within him wasn't buying it. "I don't know."

Suddenly Gino seemed to recover himself and his strength, as if some epiphany had managed to rescue him from the brink just in time. "I don't know for sure if there's someone else on this island or not," he said, his voice stronger, more even and controlled now. "Maybe there is, maybe there isn't. The odds tell me it's damn near impossible. So then it has to be that he mangled his arm on the reef and lost it once he came ashore, just like Quinn said. It's either that or someone did this to him, which means we're not alone. If it's neither of those things, then that leaves us."

"That's ridiculous," Quinn said. "None of us did this."

"Exactly my point," he said. "The only one I'd even suspect might be Herm."

"*Herm?*" Dallas laughed, but it was one of panic and disbelief, not humor. "Are you insane? As if he even *could* do something like this, much less to Andre."

"That's not what I said."

"Besides, why would Herm do such a thing? He's not capable."

"We're all capable. Besides, we're under an abnormal amount of stress, and we're struggling with thirst and food issues, it can alter a person's—"

"I don't care how thirsty he is. He's a history teacher, not Jason Voorhees."

"There was a period of time, during that first night, before we found each other. Damn near anything could've happened. An altercation, maybe, or some sort of disagreement, I—"

"Come on, Gino," Quinn said, "this is hardly the time to play devil's advocate."

"My point is that Andre's arm was lost *somehow*, and there's only a certain number of ways it could've happened. We can't know for sure at this point, but unless you want to entertain one of these other scenarios, then we go with the reef explanation as the most likely, and we move the fuck on and focus on finding him."

"Yeah," Dallas said. "Okay."

Gino's posture seemed to soften a bit, and he turned to Quinn. She gave a slow nod.

Dallas put a hand on Gino's shoulder. It was hard as granite. He knew if Gino let his emotions go—allowing himself something other than anger—he'd be better able to process what was happening, but that wasn't going to happen because that might also make him vulnerable, and in his mind, weak. A man like Gino didn't do vulnerable and weak. He knew one way, and that was strength, right or wrong. Dallas had always known how to reach him, but it wasn't foolproof, and he could only hope the usual approach would work. "We need you. I know this is fucked up, and we're all scared and confused here, all right? I'm not making sense either, I'm sorry, I—I don't understand any of this. I know you loved Andre. We all did. But we need you to hold it together, man. If you lose it, we're all fucked. Understand?"

"Listen to him," Quinn said. "We can't make it without you."

Gino looked down at the ground a moment and closed his eyes, his sculpted chest slowly rising and falling. When he opened his eyes he gave both Dallas and Quinn reassuring nods. "You guys go back to camp," he said. "Secure the water, the fire and what little else we have. Then get to work on opening some more coconuts, but not too many. They're a natural laxative. Last thing any of us needs is dysentery."

"What about you?"

"I'm gonna look for him."

"Not alone you're not," Dallas said.

"You don't have shoes," he reminded him. "You can't handle this terrain without ripping your feet to shreds. Then you'll be useless to yourself and us. Go back to camp and get things together there. I'll handle this."

"I'll go with him," Quinn said.

"Don't go too far," Dallas warned. "And be back before dark. I don't want to have to come looking for you guys."

"Worry about what I told you to do," Gino said, face set like stone. "I got this."

"What about…" Dallas motioned to the arm without looking at it. "Do we just leave it there?"

"At this point, we don't have much choice," Quinn said softly.

"We need to find his body," Gino said. "Get back to camp, look after the others."

Dallas and Quinn exchanged troubled glances and then kissed quickly. Without another word, she and Gino pushed on, vanishing into the brush and leaving Dallas alone in the clearing.

In a haze of confusion and both physical and emotional exhaustion, Dallas left the jungle and walked back across the beach, past a bevy of rotted coconuts scattered about. Less than a mile beyond the water's edge, on the far side of the coral reef that ran nearly the entire length of the island, the open sea surged with each incoming wave, slapping the reef and flying up into the air in great misting sprays. The sun, still brilliant in the blue, clear, endless sky, hung lower than it had earlier, slowly sinking into the horizon like the dispassionate deity it was.

And as Dallas headed back toward the others, the jungle watched, silent, still and predatory.

Along with whatever else was hidden within it.

CHAPTER FIVE

They followed the blood.

Swaths of it on the ground, smears all around them, and after perhaps fifty feet or so, they came across Andre's other sneaker. It too was stained with blood, and while touching it was the last thing Quinn wanted to do, when Gino told her to grab it as now they had a pair Dallas could wear, she snatched it up, ignoring the still sticky blood along the sides and soaked into the laces.

She'd seen her share of blood and gore in the past, but it was never something with which she'd become nonchalant or comfortable. Choking back bile, she pressed on, clutching the shoe and pressing it tight against the side of her chest. With each new discovery of blood, Quinn forced visions of Andre—disoriented and bleeding to death as he stumbled through the jungle—from her mind, knowing that eventually this would end with his body collapsed and long dead. There would be no miracles, not even any goodbyes. Theirs was not a mission of rescue, but recovery.

Gino stopped, crouched down and looked more closely at a

splotch of dark crimson near the base of a large stalk. He looked around but remained crouched. "It's no different than tracking any other wounded animal," he said flatly. "Body's close."

"We've gone pretty far."

"Don't worry. I know what I'm doing. We're not lost."

Quinn nodded, but despite Gino's expertise and assurances, she'd never felt more lost. Surrounded by a thick maze of stalks, plant life and brilliantly colorful flowers, giant spider webs that seemed too beautifully intricate and enormous to be real, and a strangely fragrant though oppressive heat, they may as well have been on another planet. Nothing seemed quite right here. She'd seen trees and plant life her entire life, but none like this. Even the flowers were large, bizarre, Technicolor and exaggerated, as if born from the dreams of a child. What she'd have called *exotic* in the past had since taken on an almost Wonderland feel. *Through the looking glass*, she thought. And in that moment, Quinn felt farther from reality, home and everything she'd known than ever before. Why not a vast expanse of space rather than an ocean? Why not some alien world instead of a deadly paradise of Earthly origin? It seemed just as real as anything else in this place where nothing and everything mattered, where life and death held each other so close that one could scarcely be determined from the other.

"Doesn't make any sense," Gino said with a shake of his head. He held a hand up, alerting Quinn to remain where she was, as he ventured a bit further, eyes trained on the ground. When he returned, still studying the jungle floor, his expression was even more perplexed. "Just doesn't…"

"What's wrong?"

"I've been following the blood trail because it's really hard to see footprints in this kind of terrain, too much underfoot, and the ground's firmer here than on the beach," he explained. "But if you know what to look for you can make out when there's been impact with a significant amount of weight. It disrupts the ground enough to make an impression."

Quinn hugged herself. "Okay, so what are you seeing then?"

"He fell," he said, pointing. "See the indentation in the ground? These two here, those are his knees. He dropped to his knees and then fell forward. Here. See?"

"I think so." She pictured Andre lying there. Dying, hopeless and alone in the dark and wondering where she and the others were, and why no one had come to help him. Or had he thought himself the only survivor? What had gone through his mind in those last moments while he lay dying?

"The depth of those knee marks tells me he landed hard," Gino said. "Much harder than he would've by just sinking to his knees. He didn't throw himself down that hard for no reason. Nobody does that from a stationary position anyway. That means he had a good deal of momentum behind him when his knees hit."

"He was running?"

"Yeah, he was definitely moving, and fast."

"With that wound I find it hard to believe he even made it this far without losing consciousness and bleeding out. But I guess, maybe an adrenaline dump, and he's disoriented, frightened, in shock, he starts to run and he—"

"But then he fell onto his knees and pitched forward onto his chest. Up to that point, what I'm seeing makes sense." Gino stood, bent forward at the waist and continued to study the terrain, moving forward and up a slight incline onto another shelf of jungle floor. Once there, he stood upright, hands on hips. "But..."

"What is it?" Quinn climbed up behind him.

"Up ahead, there's a much larger amount of blood, like that's where he ended up. But there's no body, which means he somehow got back up and kept going, even though there's nothing to indicate that. When I went up ahead just now, there's no more blood. The trail ends there."

"That not possible with that sort of wound. Even if he got up and kept going there has to be a blood trail right up until we find the body. There has to be."

"I know. But what I'm saying is that it stops there, with that big stain where he fell onto his stomach. From what I'm seeing, his body should be there. But it's not. It's like he got that far and then just... disappeared."

"Disappeared?"

"And that's not the only thing. It shouldn't look like this. The trail, it should have a different look."

"What does that mean?"

"See how the disturbance in the ground is more or less the same width and length it was back where it first started?" Gino pointed to a wide swath of sand, dirt, blood and flattened leaves just ahead of them. "It goes up the incline and over to that point there. Andre's body left that mark. Not his knees, not his footprints, but his body. His entire body, lying flat and bleeding out, left its mark on the ground as it went."

Quinn looked back at where they'd come from. "So he fell back there, onto his knees, then pitched forward and crawled up here? Is that what you're saying?"

"That's what makes the most sense," Gino said. "Problem is that's not what this is telling me. That's not what this looks like. It *should* look like that, but it doesn't."

"Okay, what *does* it look like?"

"The track is too smooth, steady. Same with the blood, see how it's smeared in a solid line the whole way? If he was crawling, it shouldn't look like that. The blood spatter and smear should have a little more intermittent or uneven look to it, and the track should too. Same as it would with any badly wounded animal."

"All right," she said, head spinning. "So…"

"So just like his body should be over there, but it's not, it looks…"
Brow knit, he ran a dirty hand across his face, and the several days of

beard growth there. "I mean, if this was any other injured animal I was tracking I'd swear it looks…"

"It looks *what*? For crying out loud, just tell me."

Gino's dark eyes found her. "It looks like he was dragged."

It was getting later. The sky was changing, slowly transforming into a glowing orange color, as if the world had caught fire just above the ocean. The breeze had changed too, becoming a bit cooler as it set the palm trees swaying and the edge of the jungle rustling. Herm and Dallas had fed the fire and kept it going, and it was slowly growing stronger. Though the goal was to eventually turn it into a bonfire, the flames high and spitting sparks, they hadn't gathered enough burnable material to achieve that as yet. They hoped they had enough to keep it going through the coming night, but exhaustion had gotten the better of them. The lack of water and food was bad enough, but their utter mental, emotional and physical fatigue meant that pulling anything more from the jungle simply wasn't an option until they were able to recharge.

At their makeshift camp, Murdoch was maintaining consciousness for longer periods than earlier, and Harper had taken up position a few feet away on a large piece of driftwood, weeping while unenthusiastically gnawing away at a piece of coconut Dallas had managed to crack apart after nearly half an hour of attacking it with a sharp rock. Since then he and Herm had fed on and drank from another, sharing it with Murdoch when he was alert enough to swallow without choking. The rest they left for Quinn and Gino.

There hadn't been much conversation since they'd returned to camp. Instead, they'd focused on the tasks at hand and kept to their own thoughts and fears about what they'd found of Andre. Dallas continually watched the jungle, waiting and hoping for Quinn and Gino to return safely. His thirst and hunger at least somewhat sated, he studied his hands and the bevy of small cuts and scrapes that littered both. Although the sharp rocks were somewhat effective in splitting the coconuts, they were also extremely difficult to handle and work with, and his hands showed it. With a sigh, he stood, walked down to the water's edge and soaked his hands a few moments, washing away the blood and letting the saltwater rush between his fingers.

"You think they'll find him?"

Dallas quickly looked behind him.

"Sorry," Herm said, sidling up next to him, "didn't mean to startle you."

Dallas nodded but said nothing. He didn't much feel like talking just then.

"Do you?"

"What?"

"Think they'll find him."

"I don't know, Herm."

"Between you and me," he said, crouching too, "there's something about this whole thing that doesn't add up."

Though they were clean, Dallas continued to bathe his hands in the gentle surf.

"If Andre got caught on the reef," Herm continued, "and his arm was mangled to the point that he actually lost it once he got into the jungle, then where was the blood?"

"What are you talking about? There was blood all over the place."

"In the jungle, yeah, but not leading in and none on the sand. Think about it. If his arm was barely attached when he reached shore, there would've been a huge amount of blood loss by the time he got there. And even if every trace of blood in the water or along the shore washed away in the night, there still would've been a trail of it across the sand leading to the jungle. Even that heavy rain wouldn't have washed it all away. But there wasn't. The only blood was where we found his arm."

Until that moment, Dallas had only been half-listening. But Herm's assessment hit him like a slap in the face, and he found himself wondering how he hadn't thought of that as well. He'd had his suspicions in the jungle, but this was so obvious. "Yeah, you—you've got a good point."

"I know I do." Herm scratched at the edge of his hairpiece, nonchalantly sliding a finger up and under the side of it as he scratched his head. "And what that point tells me is that Andre didn't tear his arm up on that reef out there. He lost it right where we found it, in the jungle."

Dallas was so tired and drained he couldn't think straight, and worse, he was becoming used to it. "That makes sense. Seems obvious even, but…"

"Yeah, well after everything we've been through, and the shape we're in right now, none of us are thinking all that clearly."

Dallas forced himself to focus and organize his mind into some semblance of order. "So then what happened to him?"

"Well that's just it, isn't it?"

"You say anything to Harper or Murdoch about this?"

"No, didn't see much point in it. Harper's already shutting down. Far as I can tell, she's right on the edge of a breakdown. And Murdoch's not exactly coherent yet."

Standing, Dallas rubbed his eyes. "This is insane."

"We're not alone on this island, Dal."

Dallas rubbed his wet hands across his face, letting the water trickle down along his neck and chest. A little way out, the sharks were returning, as they did each day at both dusk and dawn. "Come on, man, we—"

"Something did that to him. Either someone or a some*thing*, but it wasn't that goddamn reef. We need to get the hell out of here and—"

"And how do we do that, fly? There's nowhere to go."

"I'm telling you—"

"Easy."

"We're not alone here."

"Keep your voice down. And you don't know that."

"Yeah, I do. And so do you. I can tell. Known you too long, buddy."

"I don't have all the answers, but we need to hold it together as best we can. Don't jump to conclusions just yet."

Herm straightened up, put his hands on his hips and looked out at the ocean in what he likely considered something of a heroic pose. Though he'd wanted to appear brave and unaffected, he looked silly, like the uncertain and displaced middle-aged high school teacher he was. Theirs had always been an easy relationship, fellow teachers and casual friends outside work. And even in such extreme circumstances, Dallas still couldn't shake the Herm he knew so well, the one strolling the school hallways and wisecracking with the kids, a sad sort who presented himself as if he were popular with the students, when in fact most of them made fun of him behind his back, laughing at his wig, mocking his mannerisms and doing horrible impersonations of him.

"I'm sorry," Dallas said softly.

"What for?"

"If I hadn't invited you to come with us you'd—"

"Don't be a jackass. I wanted to come. To be honest, I was really glad you included me. I felt a little out of place being the only single one, but what else is new, right?"

"We'll get out of this. One way or another, we'll get out."

"I'm so tired," he said.

"Me too, we—we're all spent."

"My whole body aches, and half the time I can't even put together a coherent thought." Herm pushed his eyeglasses up higher onto the bridge of his nose and gazed over at camp. "I'm too old for this Gilligan's Island shit." He smiled but there wasn't much behind it, and his expression quickly turned more serious. "Maybe tomorrow we can position some rocks or coconuts into a big-ass SOS on the sand. Hey, works in the movies. We need to keep that fire going strong too, got to get it built up a lot higher, especially at night. Have to hope someone sees it and gets us out of here."

That seemed about as likely as escaping the island via spaceship, but Dallas played along. "Yeah, sure."

"Trust me, someone's going to find us," Herm insisted. "Must be shipping lanes out there or something, or maybe a plane or—whatever—point is in this day and age—"

"Not sure any of that applies here."

"Time will tell." Herm grinned smugly.

"Time's a funny thing," Dallas said. "It was always so precious. Scarce, you know? But even when it's all we have it's never enough. Right about now we've got nothing but, and it's still the enemy."

"This whole place is the enemy, you ask me. Paradise my hairy ass."

"What the hell's taking them so long out there?" Dallas turned his attention back to the jungle, as an array of horrible scenarios and possibilities coursed through his mind. "They don't show soon I'm going after them."

"You better be careful with him, my friend."

"Don't start."

"I know you and Gino are old pals and you think he's our savior and all that, but I'm telling you—"

"If it wasn't for Gino, we'd already be—"

"Blah, blah, blah, thanks, I get it. He's the Almighty out here. Good for him. You pray to him if you want, but don't expect me to."

"If you're right, and there is something else out there, we'll need him even more."

"I'm not saying he doesn't have his uses." Herm stumbled away awkwardly then came right back, as if he'd forgotten something. "But I'm telling you, as a friend myself, you better watch him."

"Meaning what, exactly?"

"Meaning this isn't like back home, okay?"

"No shit."

"The rules are changing."

"You think I don't know that?"

"If you give a guy like Gino too much power, and let him make all the rules, it can be dangerous. He's the big bad wolf, the alpha male—I get it—we're all pussies and—"

"That's not what I'm saying."

"No? Well, here's what *I'm* saying." Herm lowered his voice, but the level of intensity in his eyes was unmistakable. "Every pack has rules that all the members have to follow, even the alpha male. Know why? Because every alpha male, if he's never challenged or questioned, can just as easily destroy the pack as save it."

"We're not a pack of wolves."

"You sure?"

Dallas stared at him.

"The longer we're stuck here, Dal, the less human we're going to get."

Dallas wanted to be horrified. But he knew Herm was right. It was already happening. Maybe not in deeds or gestures, but inside each of them things were changing instinctually, adapting, searching for ways to survive and find an upper hand, a superior position if need be.

Just when he'd begun to feel hopeless, Quinn and Gino appeared on the beach, exiting the jungle at a slow and steady pace. As they headed their way, Dallas watched them, his eyes bouncing back and forth between his friend and his wife. Gino was hard to read, but he could tell from the look on Quinn's face that something was wrong.

"They're coming," he said, motioning to them.

Herm turned, his tired eyes blinking slowly behind the scratched and smudged lenses of his glasses. "Anything?" he asked when they'd gotten closer.

"No sign of the body," Gino said to Dallas, looking right past Herm. "It's like it just—I don't know—disappeared. Might've been dragged, I couldn't really tell."

"*Dragged*? By what?"

"I don't know."

"Well I came up with something I think you missed," Herm said, straightening his posture and striking another of his poses.

Gino finally looked at him. "Oh yeah, what's that?"

Herm explained the lack of blood on the beach but had only gotten a few words out when Gino interrupted him.

"Quinn just pointed that out a few minutes ago on our way back. We got it." He slapped Herm on the back, but there was no camaraderie in it. It was purposely demeaning, and they all knew it. "You worry about the fire, okay, chief?"

Something died in Herm just then, his words of becoming less human echoing in Dallas's mind. It was as if Gino had kicked him, or worse, dismissed him as not even worthy of a kick. Anger, resentment— maybe more—smoldered in Herm's eyes, but he said nothing more.

"So he lost the arm in the jungle then?" Dallas asked.

"Everything points to that," Quinn said. "But we're all tired and…"

"Then we're not alone here?"

"I don't know. Probably, but…"

"But maybe not."

"There's likely a reasonable explanation for all this," Quinn said, though it didn't sound like even she'd bought it. "We just have to find it."

Gino turned and pointed to the cliffs. "Tomorrow I'm going up there and getting a view of the island and what we're dealing with."

Quinn moved closer to Dallas. He put an arm around her shoulder. "And until then?"

"We secure camp as best we can and stay alert. Take shifts staying awake, feeding the fire and keeping watch."

Herm walked away, trudging off through the sand in a gait that would've been comical had it not been so sad.

"Come on, it'll be dark soon," Gino said. "We've got to get ready."

Night was on its way, and there'd be no stopping it.

All they could hope for now was that it planned to come alone.

Chapter Six

On the island, the darkness was unlike anything they'd experienced before. Even Gino, with all the exotic locales he'd visited in his life, had never seen anything quite like it. The night was complete and pure, and but for the stars in the heavens, void of any light whatsoever. The feel of the island changed after dark as well. Sound amplified and sharpened, each wave lapping shore, every crackle of fire, surge of wind, coconut dropping from the trees or shifting of the jungle stood out as a reminder that this was an alien place where they were the intruders. At one point they were swarmed by mosquitos and other small flying bugs, and only the smoke wafting from the fire was able to dissipate them, though only somewhat.

Snuggled together, Dallas and Quinn took up position near the fire. They were supposed to sleep until it was time for them to take watch, and Dallas was sure he had drifted off a few times, but sustaining it proved impossible. Although she didn't say anything, Dallas had slept in Quinn's arms for years and he could tell when she was restless or not fully asleep, and he knew she was experiencing the same thing. Despite their exhaustion, sleep refused to come in anything but short intervals. In its place came fear, worry and a gnawing sense of loss and longing for their lives back home.

Gino sat crouched near the fire but facing the jungle. Every few minutes he'd change position so he could keep an eye on the stretch of beach behind them as well, though it seemed unlikely he could see far in such utter blackness.

Herm and Murdoch lay a few feet away. Dallas couldn't tell for sure about Murdoch, but Herm was awake, his eyeglasses resting on his chest and his eyes open and blankly staring up at the night sky.

Sleep was not a problem for Harper however, as she was curled tightly into a fetal position, out soundly and had been quietly snoring for some time.

Dallas closed his eyes, held Quinn tight and tried not to think about home. He couldn't take it. The idea that they might never leave this place, might never again get home and see their family and friends and resume their lives, was too much to bare after everything they'd already been through. The chance—however slim—that they could make it back was the only thing that kept them from not completely losing whatever was left of their minds and spiraling down into complete breakdowns. But in the quiet, in the dark, holding the woman he loved, Dallas couldn't be sure he believed any of it. Maybe they were already dead and just didn't know it. Maybe Davis and Andre and Natalie were the lucky ones, spared the horrors of dying slowly, gradually, in a place so far from home. Maybe for Dallas and the rest of them, the nightmare was just beginning.

The next time sleep took him, before he came awake again with a start, he slipped away into a dream. Or something similar. All Dallas knew for sure was that for a brief period his body no longer ached, he was no longer so hungry or thirsty, his mind was clear and exhaustion had left him. He was himself again, safe and comfortable.

No longer lying in the sand, he was instead sitting on his back deck, gazing out at the night and the small, fenced yard. Quinn was inside, he could hear her through the screen door moving around in the kitchen.

And then something in the shadows at the edge of the deck caught his attention.

Something that wasn't supposed to be there.

Something not quite…human.

"Who's there?" he asked.

The sudden sensation of falling tore him from sleep, and he was back on the beach, Quinn's head nestled against his chest, her hair tickling his face.

Herm rolled over, stood up and began to stumble away from camp, brushing sand from his shirt as he went.

"Where are you going?" Gino asked.

"Well, since right about now I'm going through nicotine

withdrawal so bad I'd blow a fucking hobo for a Marlboro, I figured I'd hit the convenience store and get a pack of butts. Anybody else want anything?"

"I asked you a question."

Herm stopped, sighed and jerked a thumb at the ocean. "I need to take a piss. That okay with you?"

"Don't go too far."

"Aye aye, captain." Herm gave an exaggerated salute as he moved away.

"Jackass," Gino muttered.

Dallas gently freed himself from his wife's grasp then sat up. Quinn was awake too but remained curled up on the ground.

"Want me to take over?" Dallas asked Gino. "Can't sleep anyway."

"I can do a couple more hours."

Quinn propped herself up on her elbows and craned her neck for a better look at Murdoch. "Has anyone checked on him lately?"

"I'm okay," Murdoch answered quietly.

"Do you need anything?" Quinn asked.

"A nice thick juicy steak, medium rare and smothered in sautéed mushrooms. Baked potato with sour cream and chive. Lobster dripping in butter. Couple ice cold bottles of beer."

"I'll have what he's having," Dallas said.

Herm returned, noticed Harper snoring quietly nearby. "Must be nice, huh?"

"We're having surf and turf," Quinn told him, "want to join us?"

"Funny," he chuckled. "I was just thinking about Dog Heaven back home."

"Best hotdogs in town," Dallas said.

"What I wouldn't give right now for a foot-long with mustard, ketchup and relish."

"I've always been partial to their chili-dogs." Dallas closed his eyes, pictured the food in his mind. "You know what else is good there? Those seasoned fries."

"To die for!" Quinn added. "If we were there right now I'd have a dog slathered with mustard, and big order of those fries."

Gino stood up from his crouch. "What happened to the steaks and lobsters?"

"I'd go for those too," Herm said.

"What's your favorite at Dog Heaven, Gino?" Quinn asked.

"I don't eat that shit," he scoffed. "It's poison."

"Delicious poison," Herm said. "I mean, hell, a steak's not exactly the best thing in the world for you either, but that doesn't stop you from eating one does it? Besides, you ever have the onion rings at Dog Heaven, they—"

Gino silenced him, raising a hand and turning quickly in the direction of the jungle. His eyes panned back and forth then back again, through the darkness and across the jungle's edge.

"What is it?" Quinn asked, sitting up.

Rather than answer, Gino took a step toward the jungle.

"Gino?" Dallas said.

"Everybody stay here." He turned and slipped away into the darkness.

No one moved or spoke for several seconds.

Finally, Murdoch asked, "What's wrong?"

"It'll be all right," Quinn assured him in a loud whisper. "We just need to stay quiet a minute."

Suddenly the island was deathly still. Even the wind had stopped. Only the crackling motion of the fire remained, and the unrelenting darkness just beyond its flames.

Moments later, Gino separated from the darkness and emerged from a section of nearby jungle. When he rejoined the others at the fire, he was clearly perplexed, but seemed none the worse for wear.

"What's wrong?" Dallas asked.

"I don't know," Gino said, brow knit. "Nothing."

"What was that all about then?" Herm asked.

"Thought I heard something moving out there, but I guess not."

"Out where?"

"Through the brush."

"So you did or you didn't. Which is it?"

Gino moved closer to him. "I just said I thought I did but I guess I was wrong."

"*You? Wrong?* Come on, that can't be it."

An eerie calm came over Gino. There was something unsettling about it. Cold and predatory, the way a snake goes still just before it strikes.

"We're all exhausted," Dallas said. "Gino, why don't you try to get some rest, let me take watch for a while, huh?"

"I can do—"

"Yeah, I know, but let me take it anyway. Get some rest."

He continued glaring at Herm for what seemed an eternity before finally answering. "Fine."

While Gino curled up with Harper and Herm sat down in front of the fire, Quinn crawled over to Murdoch, let him know everything was all right, and then joined Dallas on watch on the other side of the flames.

"Sometimes I swear he *wants* Gino to kick his ass," Dallas whispered to her.

"One of these times you're not going to be there to save him."

"Not sure I could anyway. Gino's a powder keg."

"And Herm's the match," she whispered.

An hour or so later, Quinn had fallen asleep with her head in his lap. Dallas stayed awake, watching the jungle and the surrounding darkness as best he could. At one point, he looked behind him, saw Gino and Harper clinging to each other. Far as he could tell, both were asleep. It felt strange to see Gino exhibiting such vulnerability, and it occurred to Dallas that in all the years he'd known him, he'd never seen Gino like that before. The intensity and bravado gone, he looked like a slumbering child, innocent and without a worry in the world.

Dallas next turned his focus to Murdoch. Due to the eye injuries it was hard to tell, but he appeared to be out as well, the slow rhythm of his chest rising and falling indicative of someone soundly asleep.

Herm was still sitting on the other side of the fire, staring into the flames.

"Jesus, man, you still awake?" he asked quietly.

His eyes lifted, found him through the fire. Dallas had never seen such a look in Herm's eyes, and it was startling. Something akin to hatred had settled behind them, barely contained rage. Apparently Gino wasn't the only powder keg. "You all right?"

"Are you?" Herm returned his gaze to the flames. "Are any of us?"

Dallas never answered.

The night kept its secrets as well. And the darkness just kept coming.

As the sun broke over the horizon, the heat immediately began to rise and soon became oppressive. The island awakened and came to life along with them, but the ocean was oddly calm that morning, the usual large spraying waves crashing the reef replaced with slower, smaller breaks that were barely noticeable.

The plan for the day was that Gino and Dallas would make their way through the jungle and up onto the summit of the cliff so they could get a better look at the entire island. Meanwhile, Quinn and Herm would do their best with the few sharpened sticks they had to spear a fish or two, or at a minimum, scour the rocks along the shoreline farther down the beach for crabs or other edible crustaceans. Despite her objections and desire to join the others, Harper was to remain at camp, keep the fire going and watch over Murdoch.

In the shade of a palm tree, Dallas pulled his wife in close to him. "You going to be okay?"

Quinn smirked at him. "Come on. I can take care of myself. You know that."

"Just be careful. You know, when you're not being a badass motherfucker."

"Do my best." She raised up on her tiptoes and kissed him. "Love you."

Dallas was sure he had never loved Quinn more than he did in that moment. "Love you too. Be back in a while."

Gino's goodbye to Harper consisted of a kiss on the forehead and a quick slap on the ass. Then he motioned for Dallas to follow him and headed off. "Wrap it up, lovebirds."

"Got to go," Dallas said with the best smile he could muster.

"Watch yourself out there."

Dallas nodded, then turned and jogged along the sand until he'd caught up with Gino. They slipped into the jungle, forcing their way through the thick vegetation before heading in the general direction of the cliffs. The deeper they ventured the more rugged and difficult to negotiate the terrain became. Without the benefit of a machete or anything to cut their way through, it was difficult going, and when they finally found an incline leading up to the cliffs nearly thirty minutes later, the undergrowth was heavier than ever. They were also exhausted and bathed in sweat, so they stopped for a moment to rest.

Gino peeled off his tank top and tied it around his head into a makeshift scarf, pulling the back down to shield his neck. "There's no canopy here," he said. "Won't be the rest of the way, so try to cover your head best you can."

Dallas gave a weary nod but was too winded to remove the t-shirt he'd taken from Natalie's body. A few sizes too small, it was tight, soaked in sweat and stuck to him, but at least provided some defense from the sun.

Slick with perspiration, Gino wiped his brow, and through squinted eyes, peered through the last patch of vines and trees and heavy growth, and up at the cliffs in the distance. "Almost there," he said.

"This last leg's going to be a bitch, though."

"Definite incline, but it doesn't look too bad."

"Compared to what?"

"Trust me, I've seen and climbed far worse. This is nothing, we got lucky."

"I'm feeling lots of things right now, man. Lucky isn't one of them."

"Jungle gives way in maybe another forty yards, then it gets rocky, lots of roots and vines. Just stay close to me as you can. If you have trouble, don't be shy about it, let me know, understand? You don't want to go sliding back down this sort of terrain, those rocks up there'll take the skin right off you."

Dallas bent forward, hands on his thighs, and tried to catch his breath. He was in reasonably good shape, but he no longer possessed the physical stamina he'd always taken for granted. "I'll be sure to scream like a little girl at the first hint of danger."

"That'll work." Gino allowed a slight smile.

In the few moments of silence that followed, Dallas adjusted his sneakers. Although preferable to being barefoot, they were too big for his feet, and he couldn't look or touch them without being reminded that he was wearing his dead friend's shoes. Because of the sweat and the way his feet slid back and forth with each step, he was already getting the start of a couple blisters.

"When we get back to camp, you need to pack them," Gino said. "Shred a piece of Nat's clothes and pack the sneakers tight so your foot doesn't move inside them, or your skin's going to be raw by the end of the day."

"Okay." In the interim, he tried pulling the laces tighter. It helped somewhat. "Can I ask you something, man?"

"Anything, you know that."

"It's just us now. What do you think happened to Andre?"

"What do you think?"

Surprised he'd asked, Dallas thought a moment before answering. "I don't think it was a shark and I don't think the reef had anything to do with it. Whatever happened took place in the jungle where we found his arm. I don't know anything beyond that, but that much I'm convinced of. And if I'm right, then we're not alone here."

"Problem is I haven't been able to come up with anything that makes sense, and until we know for sure, it's just another farfetched maybe I can't get my head around."

"Fucking madness," Dallas sighed.

They went quiet again.

"You scared?" Gino finally asked.

"Since the first storm forced us into the water. Aren't you?"

Gino slowly shook his head. "If there's something out there, it needs to fear me."

He believed him. Because just then, the look in Gino's dark eyes made Dallas fear him too. Oddly, he found comfort in that.

"Come on, let's move," Gino said. "We sit here too long we'll bake in this sun."

"Right behind you, boss."

As Gino started up and into the last stretch of jungle, Dallas looked back in the direction they'd come. More than once he'd felt as if he and Gino weren't the only ones moving around out here, and although he'd stayed alert, he never said a word about it. If Gino hadn't sensed anything, with all his training and experience, then surely there was nothing to worry about. Or had he sensed it too and kept it to himself? Dallas wondered. But he was already lagging behind, so he pushed those concerns from his mind and started through the tangle of vegetation toward the summit of the cliff.

Back at camp, Quinn had just finished tending to Murdoch's wounds, cleaning and drying them, when he blinked rapidly with his right eye, which was the less damaged of the two. His breath caught in his throat as he reached out and took her by the shoulders, awkwardly, gently. "My God," he said softly.

"What is it?"

"I can see. Not well, you're blurry, but I can see you."

Quinn smiled. Finally, some good news. "That's wonderful," she said, taking his shoulders as well. "Now rest and try to keep that area clean as you can."

"Getting tired of being useless around here. I'm the skipper, I—"

"You'll do more good once you've fully recovered. You're doing miraculously well, don't blow it now by overdoing. Rest. Doctor's orders."

Murdoch slumped back, dropped his arms and sat in the sand. "Yes, ma'am."

As Quinn regained her feet, Herm appeared, his tattered jeans rolled up to his knees and his undershirt already soaked in sweat. In his hand he held a makeshift spear. With his wig and scratched eyeglasses, he looked like something that had wandered out of a comedy sketch.

"I'm going to head down to the rocks and see if I can find any edibles," he said. "Comedic gold aside, I think our odds for success are a lot better going that route than wading around out there trying to spear a fish."

"Agreed. I'll join you."

Harper, who had just tossed a few sticks onto the fire, sauntered over to them and with a dramatic sigh said, "Can I come too?"

"You need to stay here and watch the fire."

"It's not like it'll go out if we leave it alone for a couple minutes."

Herm rolled his eyes and strode down to the waterline, following it in the direction of the rocks and caves farther down the beach.

"I also don't want Murdoch left alone," Quinn said, lowering her voice.

"Didn't he just say he could see or whatever?"

"We all have jobs to do, Harper. Yours is to tend the fire and watch over camp."

Harper clamped her hands on her tiny waist. "It's boring as fuck here, I—"

"You heard what Gino said."

"Yeah, well no offense, *lady*, but you're not the boss of me and neither is Gino, okay? I'm sick of everyone telling me what to do like I'm a little kid or something."

"Look, *princess*," Quinn snapped, "this shit is the last thing I need right now."

"I thought you were dope but now you're just acting like a bitch."

Quinn stared at her.

"Whatever. It's not like I want to go with Herm anyways," Harper said, twirling the ends of her hair with a finger. "You can go with that perv if you want, I don't care. I'm sick of him staring at me all the time. He thinks I don't know he's doing it, he thinks he's all slick or whatever, but I know he stares at me all the time, I keep catching him. And I know what he's thinking too. And, um, *gross*."

Quinn felt a headache settling behind her eyes. Maybe it was just hunger, the heat and sun. She could only hope. "Keep that to yourself. There's already enough tension between Herm and Gino. We don't need—"

"Don't be a retard. Like I'd say something to Gino. OMG, he'd kill him. You don't even know how jealous he gets sometimes. If he knew what Herm was doing—"

"Herm's harmless. I'm sure he doesn't mean anything by it."

"He's just got you fooled 'cause he's not staring at *your* tits all day and night." She shrugged, standing there in her little bikini, which had become filthy and worn and with the passing of each day, left less and less to the imagination. "Can I at least take a spear and try to catch us some fishes?"

Had there been any humor left in her, Quinn likely would've burst out laughing. Instead, she sighed and said, "Knock yourself out. Just don't go too far and make sure you keep an eye on the fire and Murdoch, okay? Herm and I'll be back in a little while."

Nat and Andre are dead and this useless bitch is still alive, she thought. It felt foreign and ugly and not something she'd normally think, much less believe, but it sprang into Quinn's mind suddenly and without warning. They were all spiraling down more and more each day, each hour, each moment. Farther and farther away from who they had once been and still believed themselves to be. Quinn had never been a violent person, yet she found her anger and annoyance toward Harper turning quickly to a desire to hurt her, to strangle her by her scrawny neck, to punch her in that brainless head and to shut that big mouth by whatever means necessary.

"What?" Harper asked her. "Why are you looking at me like that?"

Without answering, Quinn turned and headed down the beach.

❖

"Take my hand," Gino said breathlessly, reaching down to him. "I'll pull you up."

With the sun behind him, all Dallas could see of Gino was a silhouette, and a hand reaching down through the glare. Hanging on for dear life at the edge of the rock summit, he was too tired and worn to pull himself up, but frightened to let go long enough to grab Gino's hand. If he missed or their hands slipped, he'd slide more than a hundred yards down across terrain that would certainly badly injure and possibly even kill him. But he couldn't hold on indefinitely either.

"I got you," Gino promised, planting his feet. "Come on. Take it."

Dallas lurched toward him, throwing his hand up, and Gino grabbed him, catching him by the wrist, which given the perspiration covering both, made for a better grip. With strength and confidence, Gino pulled him up.

As he let go and fell onto the platform at the summit of the cliff, Dallas lay there a moment, sweating and exhausted and happy to have made it in one piece. "Thanks, man," he said when he'd caught his breath.

Gino, still bent at the waist and catching his breath too, said, "We got this."

"Getting back down's gonna be fun."

He stood upright and moved across the uneven top of the cliff closer to the edge. Dallas regained his feet and joined him. Never a fan of heights, it was only then that he realized just how high they'd climbed. Without question the highest point on the island, he guessed they were at about four hundred feet. From here, the ocean looked endless, even larger and more ominously beautiful than it did from shore. And the sky was so big and vast it didn't seem real.

"Christ," Dallas said, "we really are in the middle of nowhere, aren't we?"

"It's beautiful though."

"Not when it's trying to kill you."

"Even then."

Dallas looked down at the beach below. In the distance he could see camp, the fire, Murdoch and Harper near the fire, and Herm and Quinn down by the rocks.

"It's like we can see the whole world from here," Gino said.

"Ours anyway."

"That's the only one that counts these days."

They moved across the summit to get a better view of the island behind them. Unlike the ocean and sky, the island appeared much smaller than Dallas suspected it might. Likely volcanic in origin, it was perhaps four miles long and roughly five hundred yards wide, eighty or ninety-some-odd acres mostly surrounded by large rock clusters and coral reef. There was nothing but jungle until the far side of the island, where they were able to make out more beach and what appeared to be a small lagoon. Unlike on their side of the island, the rocky shoreline and reef was absent.

And then, in one section of jungle not far from the opposite side of the island, they saw something neither could immediately comprehend. Was it a hallucination, a trick of the sunlight and their exhaustion, or was it real?

"Do you...Do you see that?" Dallas muttered, pointing.

Gino shielded his eyes with his hand.

"Gino..."

"I see it."

"What do you think it—"

"We have to get back to the others," Gino said. "Now."

"Yeah," Dallas replied, unable to look away from what he was seeing.

This changed everything.

CHAPTER SEVEN

"What?" Quinn shook her head, as if hopeful it might dislodge and free her of the information she'd just received. "*Buildings*? You're sure?"

"A whole cluster of them in a cleared section of jungle," Gino told her.

"So there's people here?" Harper asked hopefully. "They can help us!"

"Jesus," Herm moaned. "Doesn't anyone have a shiny red ball she can play with while the adults talk?"

Harper, wide-eyed and confused as ever, looked at him for further explanation.

"Shut-up, asshole," Gino snapped.

"They looked like they'd been abandoned years ago," Dallas said, dismissing them both. "Even at that distance it was obvious they were falling apart."

"Amazing," Quinn said. "At some point there really were others here."

"Okay, but they're not here now though?" Harper asked.

"No, Harper." Gino sighed, as even his patience with her was waning. "They're not here now."

"Then who cares?" With a pout she stamped her foot in the sand. "WTF?"

"Excuse me, Illustrious Grand Poobah?" Herm raised his hand. "May I speak?"

"Just say your piece, idiot."

"It's most likely an old Japanese encampment of some sort," Herm explained. "Probably dates back to World War II, and it's likely been abandoned since. I can't imagine anyone else being way out here. Actually, I'm trying to figure out what they'd have been doing here too, but they're the most logical choice."

Murdoch, who had joined them, agreed. "I'm surprised the Japs would've wanted this rock too. No strategic advantage really being this far out. Can't land a plane here, difficult to get to, hell of time getting on and off of it, and unless there's something I missed, nothing of any real value here. Still, about all that makes sense. Hell, this place isn't even on the maps, and that's rare today. I've lived and made my living in these waters for years, and until we wound up here I'd have sworn on a stack of Bibles there wasn't any land out here until you hit Antarctica, and that ain't exactly right around the corner, folks."

"We couldn't see the entire layout," Dallas said, sipping some water from their dwindling supply. "There's a lagoon, and it looked like the reef didn't extend all the way around to that side of the island. The buildings are less than a mile from the beach. They look really old and rundown, but they're still standing. Or at least the ones we could see are."

Quinn knit her brow. "I know this sounds crazy, but I remember reading about Japanese soldiers who were found on a few remote South Pacific islands long after the war was over. They didn't realize it wasn't still going on and had no idea of the date. Could...I mean...Andre... maybe..."

"You think some crazy old Japanese solider is running around out there?"

Gino chuckled, though there was little humor in it. "You're kidding, right?"

"It's happened before," Quinn said.

"Herm?" Dallas motioned to him. "You're the history teacher."

"That I am, but you guys need a lesson in math, not history."

"Dipshit's finally got something right," Gino said, taking a drink of water. "They'd be way too old by now."

"While I hate to admit math might somehow be one of Gino's strong suits, he's correct. Even if we went out on a limb and assumed a soldier serving on this island was somehow left behind, and was only a teenager at the time, let's say fifteen—he'd have likely been a few years older than that, at a minimum, but for the sake of argument we'll go with that—World War II ended on September 3, 1945. It's 2014. That's sixty-nine years ago. Meaning even if we make our soldier the unlikely age of fifteen in 1945, today he'd be at least eighty-four years old. So unless we have a cranky senior citizen who wants us off his lawn, odds are that's not the answer."

They remained quiet a while. Andre was on everyone's mind, but there was nothing more to say, nothing that could erase or in any way soften the sight of his severed arm lying in the jungle. A warm breeze filled the silence, blowing in off the ocean with an eerie sound they'd become accustomed to.

"How far away are the buildings from here?" Murdoch asked. "The island's maybe four miles long and five to six football fields wide," Gino said. "So we're talking roughly six hundred yards of jungle and we'll run right into them."

"There's no telling what might be there," Quinn said, "or what they may have left behind that could be of use to us. There might even be food."

"The Japanese had MREs similar to what Americans had," Herm told them.

"Would they still be edible after all these years?"

"Some would. Theoretically at least, provided they remained sealed."

Quinn and Herm's trip to the rocks hadn't yielded anything other than a few tiny crabs and a small conch shell that turned out to be empty. Harper's attempt at spearing a fish was even less successful, which left them with the few bits of coconut they had left over from the last one they'd split.

"At this point I think I'd eat almost anything," Quinn said.

"Yeah," Herm agreed, "these coconuts are giving me the exploding shits."

Harper winced. "Way too much information thanks!"

"It's not funny," Gino said. "We're starving and almost out of water. With all the energy Dal and I already expended today, we don't get hold of some drinkable water and serious protein, we're going to be in trouble."

"No one said it was funny." Herm took up a sharpened stick. "You see anybody laughing?"

Dallas, who had sat down to relax a bit, stood up and stretched. "Let's get on with it. We stand around here talking about it all day, it'll be nightfall before we know it. We need to get to that camp soon as possible and see what's there."

"Absolutely," Gino said. "Because we're also talking about potential shelter. It may not be perfect, but it has to beat the open beach or those caves."

Quinn reached out, put a hand on Murdoch's shoulder. "John, I'm not sure you're ready for that kind of hike yet. Especially given the terrain and the thickness of the jungle. How are you feeling?"

Murdoch's expression left no doubt as to his level of frustration.

Though the wounds to his eyes had been cleaned relatively well given the circumstances, there was still dried and caked blood covering one eye (which continued to ooze a clear fluid from its corner), and a series of deep scratches and contusions littering his face. "Vision's getting better in the one eye, and I'm stronger than before, I—I can make it. Don't worry about me."

"Q, you're the one with medical experience," Gino said. "It's your call."

"No," Murdoch said, staggering toward him and nearly losing his balance in the sand before managing to right himself. "I'm a grown man, and now that my head's clearer and I'm up on my own two feet, I'll make my own decisions. And remember, son, I'm Captain, this is my party. You've just been borrowing it."

"Not sure I'd be bragging about that right now," Herm said.

He spun toward him, or perhaps just the sound of his voice. "Hell you mean by that? You got something on your mind, wig-boy?"

Harper burst out laughing, covering her mouth with her hands far too late.

"Go fuck yourself, Murdoch." Herm self-consciously adjusted his wig then seemed to realize he was doing it and quickly dropped his hands. "If it wasn't for you we wouldn't even be in this mess."

"You're out of your goddamn mind!"

"If you knew what the hell you were doing you would've gotten away from that storm instead of running us right into it. We hired you

116

with the understanding we'd be safe, that you knew your job."

"I was doing my *job* when you were in high school, boy!"

"Then you'd think you'd know enough to get your passengers out of harm's way and to safety instead of sinking your piece of shit boat and nearly killing us all."

Murdoch clenched his fists and raised them. "If it wasn't for me we'd all be dead! None of us would've even made it into the water!"

"Dream on, you fucking cretin."

"I lost a good man out there, a friend, I—"

"Enough!" Dallas growled, silencing them both. "We can't all go anyway. Someone has to stay behind and keep the fire going and watch over what little water we have left."

"Dal's right," Gino said. "We'll probably move our camp there once we've scoped it out, but for now, we need to make sure that fire stays alive. Harper, you and Murdoch stay behind and watch over things."

"But, baby, I don't want—"

"Goddamn it, just do what I tell you to do!"

Harper stomped off through the sand, pouting like a reprimanded preteen.

After an awkward moment, Dallas said, "The rest of us should get moving."

"We need to get something straight first."

Dallas already knew what was coming. "Let it go," he said quietly.

"Murdoch, long as we were on your boat, you were in charge," Gino told him. "But I run shit now. I'm not borrowing anything. You understand me? You're feeling better, and I'm glad, but there's only one captain here now, and it's me."

"Oh, for Christ's sake," Quinn moaned. "Do we really have to stand here and watch you two shake your cocks at each other?"

Gino's eyes remained locked on Murdoch. "You got me, old man?"

Murdoch stood there, shaking with anger.

"He heard you," Quinn answered for him.

"Good." Gino quickly rummaged through the four or five sharpened sticks they'd made, grabbed one then addressed those coming with him. "Try your best to conserve your energy, the heat's rising and we're almost out of water. It'll be tough going straight through the jungle, but it's not all that far. Still, there's no telling what we might run into between here and there."

"Or once we get there," Dallas added.

Gino nodded. "Or once we get there."

Using the stick as best he could, Gino took point, leading the way and slashing at the brush as they worked their way through the jungle. Some patches were quite thick and overgrown, while others were less so and easier to negotiate, but it was tough going throughout. Light trickled down through the canopy of vegetation overhead, and occasionally they'd reach areas where it was open and the sunshine shone bright and illuminating. Visibility was limited regardless, no more than a few feet at most even in the less congested sections of jungle. But they kept moving, the beach behind them becoming more distant with each passing moment.

Dallas had hoped they'd already be there by now, but he was learning how deceiving the jungle could be. It was easy to lose one's direction and sense of time and place here, and if you didn't pay close attention to everything around you, the terrain began to look the same. One could wander in circles in this jungle for hours and never realize it.

"You sure we're going in the right direction?" Herm asked at one point, huffing and out of breath.

When Gino didn't answer, Dallas said, "We've got to be getting close."

"Are you sure?"

"Just keep moving," Gino grunted.

"God," Quinn said, "it's *so* hot."

Dallas, who was in the rear, gripped his makeshift spear tight and did his best to negotiate around potential hazards, his eyes open for any threats. Again, he found himself feeling as if he and the others were not alone in the jungle.

They'd made it a bit farther when Quinn stopped, reached back and touched her husband's shoulder. He came to an abrupt halt. "What is it?"

"Did you hear that?" she asked softly.

"Hold up," he said, and when Gino and Herm stopped, he listened a moment. The breeze had either ceased or couldn't reach them here, and except for their labored breath, the jungle seemed unusually quiet.

"I could've sworn…"

"I don't hear anything," Dallas said. "What was it?"

Quinn's eyes panned slowly back and forth at the section of jungle behind them and from which they had just come. "I don't know. I thought I heard something."

"Like what?" Gino looked back over his shoulder.

"Sounded like there was someone coming up behind us."

They listened.

"It's gone now," Quinn told them. "But I…I know I heard *something*."

"I've had a strange feeling for a while now," Dallas said. "Like we're not alone."

Gino still had his tank top tied around his head. He pulled it free, wiped his face and neck down then tucked it into the waist of his shorts. "We need to keep moving."

"Yeah, we're burning daylight here," Herm said, his annoyance—

or perhaps his fear—barely contained. "Got enough to deal with. Can't keep stopping and worrying about every little sound. We're in a jungle. There's living things here. Sometimes they move around and make noise."

"Let's go." Gino pressed on. The others followed without comment.

Moments later they were met by a warm breeze filtering through the jungle and bringing with it the smell of ocean.

"Feel that? Smell it?" Gino drew in a deep breath. "We're close."

Dallas looked up ahead, and through the jungle, perhaps forty yards away, he was able to make out a large clearing and a series of buildings beyond. Shocking from the cliffs, this close there was something even more surreal about it, an outpost abandoned for decades, a remnant of those who had resided here decades ago, on an island no one knew existed.

They stopped, waited. For what, no one was sure.

"Come on," Gino eventually said, glancing back at the others before pushing his way through the final few feet of jungle.

With caution, they all stepped into the open, exhausted and bathed in sweat.

Though the jungle had taken back a good portion of what had been the encampment—including a few of the smaller buildings— the rest, though badly weathered and in various stages of dilapidation, remained essentially untouched. Debris, including large pieces of twisted metal and scattered remnants of what might have been furniture at one time lay scattered about, and what appeared to have been a Jeep-like vehicle sat half buried in a ditch that ran along the outer edge of the camp. Badly burned, the frame had since rotted and rusted.

"This is a lot bigger than I expected," Quinn said. "It's kind of creepy."

Dallas looked around at the scattered fragments and general destruction that constituted many of the buildings. Several had sustained damage beyond what time and the elements could've caused, and had suffered some sort of fire damage. "Did they bomb this place?"

"I don't think so." Gino wandered deeper into the settlement. "There's no damage to the jungle around it, and there wouldn't be this much still standing if they had. Looks like maybe they tried to burn parts of it though. From the looks, the rest were just trashed, gutted and abandoned."

"If they were leaving the island," Herm said, looking around, "it stands to reason they'd try to destroy the place on the way out. Wouldn't want anything falling into enemy hands. Then again, doesn't look like they left too much behind anyway."

Originally, the encampment had consisted of six buildings, all made largely from materials likely found on the island. Elaborate huts, mostly, but one building, set in the center of camp, was not only the largest, but also the most extensive, and appeared to have been constructed almost entirely of brick and other materials the builders would've had to import from elsewhere. Of all the buildings, it was in the best shape. Two of the smaller structures were barely standing and had been retaken by the jungle. Wrapped and mostly hidden in thick vines and growth, they were beyond entering or exploring further without extensively clearing and cutting back jungle. The three remaining buildings were more basic in terms of construction, though one sported the remnants of what had been a porch of sorts.

In the center of camp, there stood a barren flagpole.

"Was definitely some sort of military outpost," Gino said.

"Murdoch was right," Herm answered. "Had to be the Japanese. There wouldn't be anyone else out here back then or since. No point, really."

Dallas looked to a row of palm trees on the far side of the clearing, and the small stretch of beach and lagoon beyond. "What would've been the point then?"

"Who knows?" Herm said. "Must've had some strategic purpose."

"We got to check these buildings out," Gino said, "but with the exception of this big brick bastard here, none of them look that safe, so let's be careful and stay alert."

The building with the remains of a porch appeared to be living quarters. Once certain the steps were sturdy enough to hold their weight, they ventured up and onto what was left of the porch. The doorway was open, whatever door had existed years before long gone now. Inside it was mostly dark.

"What do you think?" Dallas asked. "Barracks maybe?"

"No, but definitely living quarters." Herm was the first to cross the threshold and step inside. "My guess is the commanding officer's quarters. It's nicer and bigger than the others. Barracks would have a more open layout."

A desk with one of the legs broken had left it tilted at an odd angle, not far inside the entrance, the floor covered with sand and dirt, leaves and debris. There were also numerous old papers, files and drawers and such scattered about.

"Probably an office here," Herm explained. "With the living quarters in the back."

Moving carefully, they ventured deeper inside, and came across what had been a bedroom. An old bed lay eerily positioned against one wall, still covered with sheets now faded and filthy and littered with slashes and holes. More debris and trash covered the floor, and the windows, while shuttered, were mostly blown out or open. Additional pieces of furniture and a military-style trunk lay strewn across the room.

"Look." Dallas pointed to a Japanese flag, the rising sun, faded and in tatters, hanging on one wall.

"Amazing," Herm said softly. "Empire of the Sun."

"Even after all these years," Quinn said, "you can almost feel them here."

Gino inspected the area then moved back toward the door.

124

"Structurally it seems in pretty good shape. It'll provide shelter a hell of a lot better than what we have now."

As they moved back onto the porch, Dallas motioned to the other buildings. "Okay, Herm, what's your take on the rest of this place?"

Enjoying his role as the resident expert, he grinned and strolled back down the steps, taking it all in. "My guess is those other two buildings are barracks. The bigger one to house troops, the smaller one used for officers. The two that are overgrown with jungle were likely used for storage. Again, a guess—albeit an educated one—but I'd say one for munitions and the other to store food and various supplies."

"Great," Quinn groaned. "Those are the ones we need to get into."

Gino pointed to the largest structure in the settlement, the brick building at its center. "And what about this big bastard?"

Herm pulled his glasses free, wiped perspiration from his eyes and gave a heavy sigh. "I'd say that's probably the key."

"To what?"

"Whatever the hell it was they were doing out here."

Harper and Murdoch stood side-by-side before the fire. Neither had spoken in a while until, without subtly, Harper scratched at her crotch and confessed, "I'd do some really crazy shit right now for a hot shower, I swear to God."

If Murdoch found any humor in what she'd said, he gave no indication. Instead, he stared into the flames with his good eye, entranced. "We need to get off this island."

"Duh, Captain Obvious, but how?"

"We need to find a way. Build a raft, something. We don't, we'll die here."

"You don't think they'll ever find us?"

"Girlie, I wouldn't bet that bouncy little butt of yours they're even looking anymore."

Harper left her crotch alone and hugged herself despite the heat. "For real?"

"Your boyfriend thinks he knows what he's doing. He doesn't. We're not careful, he and that damn fool with the wig are gonna get us all killed."

"Herm's gross and kind of a jerk. Gino's really smart, though."

A short burst of barking laughter escaped him. "Compared to who?"

"Huh?"

"Sweet Jesus, Mary and Joseph, woman, do you speak English?"

"Of course I do." Baffled, Harper stared at him as if his weathered face might yield clues. "What do you think I'm speaking right now?"

"Christ Almighty." Murdoch sighed, rubbed the back of his

neck. "It's gonna get worse, that's what I'm trying to tell you. I've been down but I've been listening, paying more attention than you all think. We've only been stuck here a few days and things are already breaking down, people infighting and jockeying for position, for power. We're here long enough, things are gonna go from bad to worse. Ain't gonna be any rules except for those the strongest make."

"Gino's the strongest. He'll protect me."

"Maybe so, but I need to get my strength back before it's too late."

"Too late for what?"

"To survive each other. There's no one on this island but us. Get that through your pretty little head, missy. Whoever was here years ago is long gone."

"What about what happened to Andre?"

"We don't really know *what* happened to him, now do we?"

She shrugged, her eyes glistening. "I just want to go home."

"You and me both, kid, but I'm trying to warn you that—" Murdoch's legs suddenly buckled and he let out a raspy groan.

Catching him in time, Harper helped him down onto the sand. "You okay?"

"Goddamn it, I—I'm still not myself, I…"

Harper gave his shoulder a quick pat. "Just…like…chill."

"I'm fine," he said, waving her off. "Just got a little dizzy is all."

With a shrug, she moved away and down to the water. She

removed her sneakers, emptied dirt and sand from them then let the water wash her bare feet a while.

Frustrated, Murdoch drew a deep breath and tried to calm his nerves. He was a man used to being in charge and in control of himself and others. Weakness had never been something he accepted in himself or anyone else, and since this nightmare began he'd felt nothing but. *Weak and useless*, he thought. His mind raced as his thoughts turned to Gino. That sonofabitch. Were it not for his injures and sapped strength, he'd have shown him what this *old man* could do. Arrogant bastard. Murdoch had brawled his way through some of the most dangerous ports and bars in the world. Like he was about to take orders from some punk like that. *Soon*, he thought, *I'll be back on my feet and that's when I'll make my move.*

A strange smell wafted all around him. Like a combination of rancid garbage and an oddly human smell, one of hideous perspiration and bodily fluids, it drifted down from the jungle and across the sand, assaulting his senses like a slap to the face.

Murdoch turned toward the smell and pawed quickly at his good eye. Damn vision was still terrible, but he could make out a vague outline of the palm trees and stretch of sand between his position and the jungle.

Suddenly, something large separated from the ground, materializing in a burst of dirt and flora that resembled a huge puff of smoke. It was as if the figure had been expelled and vomited forth by the earth itself, materializing before him like a nightmare.

"The *hell?*" Murdoch muttered, squinting in an attempt to bring whatever this was into better focus. But his vision wasn't strong enough to reveal further detail. He rubbed at his eye and looked again, to make sure he wasn't hallucinating. He knew damn well dehydration and lack of food could lead to—

A strange growl emanated from the shape. Human, or something similar.

Heart pounding, Murdoch struggled to his feet and looked behind him. It took him a moment to find her, but he was eventually able to make out Harper, sitting in about ankle-deep water, not far from shore.

The growl became a raspy howl, as if whoever was making it had either been screaming for hours, or hadn't made a sound in a very long time.

Murdoch spun back in its direction, nearly losing his balance.

The shape was running right for him, the glare of sun and Murdoch's limited vision conspiring to conceal what it truly was, even as it appeared to raise something above its head and increase speed, closing on him in seconds.

He wanted to say something, to call for help or to return this thing's howl with one of his own. He wanted to run right at it, fists clenched and at the ready to defend himself, to the death if need be. He wanted to do many things, but only had time to stand there, stunned and confused, as the figure swung what it was holding over its head down and across him in a rapid sweeping motion. All Murdoch saw was an odd glint of white light as sun caught steel, and then the breath snagged in the base of his throat and he tasted blood and bile. As his brain registered he'd been struck with something, hard, deep and with a savage precision he'd have never believed possible, the pain arrived, exploding through him like electrical current.

And then everything stopped. Time, sound, everything.

Vomit and blood filled his mouth, spilling free and spraying forth as the world tilted and spun. He collapsed and hit the sand. Above him, the sky, so beautiful and vast, was alive somehow, he was sure of it. Yet in that strangely horrific moment, Murdoch found himself wondering if there really was anything up there. Was God looking down upon him, watching these final moments, or was he alone, dying beneath an empty and soulless sky?

Right before he died, Murdoch thought he heard something in the distance, a scream, perhaps. But it sounded impossibly far away, and he was already drifting even further from it, gliding into the welcoming darkness.

Blood flowed to sand, turning it black with death.

CHAPTER EIGHT

Water, earth and insect life had gotten inside the other huts and buildings, causing various degrees of damage, including a mossy growth on the walls, ceilings and floors. In some cases, the jungle itself—vines and plant life—had invaded the structures, but the main building, the large brick centerpiece of the camp, was sealed off and likely more pristine inside.

Gino ran a hand over the door, a metal slab with a pull ring used to open it and a lock built directly into its face. It stood closed and was taller than he was by at least a foot. The door, dirty, rusted and dented in several places, was otherwise intact. With more effort than he'd anticipated he'd need, he was eventually able to pry the ring loose and pull it outward, providing him with a strong grip.

"If it's locked we'll never get in there," Dallas said.

"Even if it isn't," Gino muttered, bracing himself and bending his knees, "this thing is stuck solid after all these years."

After a few attempts he was able to get the door to budge, but only slightly, so using the point of his stick, Gino scraped along the frame, clearing away caked dirt, rust and debris until he'd forced most of it free.

Because of the heat and his waning strength, he had to sit a while. Then he tried again, and this time, managed to yank the door open three or four inches. The bottom scraped and caught along the cement slab positioned beneath it, so Dallas squatted down and helped, clearing it as best he could. Taking hold of the door's edge with both hands, together with Gino, who was still manning the ring, he pulled with everything he had.

Although they couldn't get it completely open, they'd gotten it three quarters of the way there, enough for them to pass.

A stale smell drifted from inside.

Gino looked inside but couldn't see a thing. Without any light to guide them, the darkness inside the windowless building was simply too great. "We'll need fire before we can go in there," he said. "Too dark otherwise."

Taking the lead, Gino crossed the remainder of the clearing and headed for the palm trees and beach beyond. The others followed, but none were prepared for what awaited them. While the other side of the island was more open and had a beach that went on for long stretches, this area was smaller and more secluded, like a secret oasis born of the surrounding jungle.

"My God," Quinn said softly, "it's beautiful."

132

GREG F. GIFUNE

The beach, narrow and no longer than a mile or so, was dotted with coconut palms swaying in the warm breeze. At its center lay a small and peaceful lagoon. While the coral reef didn't extend all the way around the island, a good distance out, rock formations protruded from the water to create a partial barrier to the ocean beyond. The constant roar of the sea remained but sounded distant and far less intrusive here.

"If we're going to head back and bring fire and the rest of the camp here," Dallas said, "we better get moving."

"Have we already decided that's happening?" Herm asked.

Dallas scratched at his growing beard. "Don't you think it makes a lot more sense to make camp here?"

"It might be a little more comfortable, but—"

"A little? We have shelter here, and it's potentially a hell of a lot safer too."

"This is the back side of the island. The tide brought us in on the other side."

"So?"

"So maybe whoever's out there looking for us is going to look there. But here, they easily could miss us. The beach is much bigger there, which means it's easier to see from the air or even from a greater distance at sea. Here, not as much."

Gino pointed to the ocean. "You see that? That's the same fucking ocean that's on the other side of the island. Hell's wrong with you? We go back, we make some torches to bring the fire, we gather

133

what little we have and we move things here. We have shelter, possibly supplies and definitely access to more things we can use. Not to mention that lagoon's going to make fishing a whole lot easier too. At least until we figure things out, this is the place to be."

"Says you."

"Yeah, Herm, says me."

"Maybe I'll stay put. I can tend to the fire there and—"

"Herm, come on," Dallas said, "splitting up isn't the answer. Besides, you know more about this place than the rest of us put together."

"I don't know anything about this place, Dal."

"You know what I mean."

"I'm not sure I do, actually."

"Do you have to argue about everything?" Quinn stepped closer to Herm, leaving no question as to whom she was addressing. "I mean, seriously, is there *any* topic you're agreeable on these days?"

"This place." Herm looked back at the buildings. "It feels... *wrong*."

"Wrong," Gino echoed.

"Yes, wrong. I don't have a good feeling about it. I don't know why, I just don't."

Quinn sighed and rubbed her eyes. She was hot, hungry and thirsty, and wanted nothing more than to find some shade and lay down a while. "I know what you mean. Like I said before, it is kind of creepy. But it's better than being out in the open, Herm."

134

"Yeah, I—you're right, I—sorry, I guess I—I'm so goddamn hungry I'm having trouble thinking straight."

"We're all hungry," Gino interrupted. "Strap on a pair and hold it together."

"That reminds me, I have something for you." Herm reached into the pocket of his jeans and came back with his middle finger held high and aimed directly at Gino. "Here you go. Enjoy."

Gino pushed by him, making sure to bump Herm none-too-gently with his shoulder as he did so. "Let's head back and get the others. Sooner we get settled in here the faster we can try to find some food."

Quinn followed, but Dallas held back, staying with Herm. "Obviously Gino can be an asshole about it," he said quietly, "but he's right. Got to keep it together. We all do."

"I'm well aware of what I need to do, Dal."

"Not looking for a fight. Just trying to be your friend."

Embarrassed, Herm looked at the ground.

"What's got you so rattled?" Dallas asked.

Rather than answer, he asked a question of his own. "You think they're still looking for us?"

"I hope so. You were sure of it yesterday. What happened?"

"I guess I'm not so sure of anything anymore." Herm motioned to the camp. "Whatever the Japanese were doing out here, it wasn't anything good. Whatever they were up to, it was something they were trying to hide, something they didn't want anyone else to know. There's no other reason for them to have been out this far, or to have built that kind of structure on an island that's uncharted to this day."

"What do you think it was?"

"No idea. But I'm not so sure us going in there and disturbing things that have been left undisturbed for decades is the way to go."

"Look, whatever went on here happened decades before you and I were even born. The people who were here and whatever the hell they were doing are distant memories now. Ghosts, man. Just ghosts."

As a warm breeze drifted across the lagoon, Herm offered the saddest little smile Dallas had ever seen. Neither spoke again. Instead, they told themselves as many lies as they needed to hear, then headed back into the waiting jungle.

After the screams, the confusion and terror, after the shock, tears and denial, an eerie quiet fell over them as they struggled to make sense of what they'd come across upon their return to the other side of the island. They were now faced with a harsh and horrifying reality they could no longer dismiss or attempt to explain away. They were not alone on the island, and whoever—whatever—was here with them, was anything but friendly.

Harper was in such shock she could barely speak, and had been

unable to explain what she'd seen or what had happened. She simply
sat beneath a nearby tree and stared off into space, tears streaming her
face. Since Gino was fixated on the body rather than Harper, Quinn had
tried to comfort her, but holding her only seemed to make the crying
worse, so she left her alone and returned to the carnage in the sand.

Murdoch's body had been cut clean in two, diagonally above
the waist. There was so much blood it almost looked staged, as it didn't
seem possible that much could have come from a single body. At first
glance the corpse didn't even look human, rather more like a mannequin
that had somehow come apart. But an exposed section of severed spine
protruding from the top half of the body, combined with a trail of
viscera and entrails slimy and slick and soaked in even more blood, left
no doubt that what they were looking at was not only a dead body, but
one that had been slaughtered.

Quinn joined Gino, who had crouched down closest to the
horror, his hand over his nose and mouth to ward off the stench, and
forced herself to take a closer look at the massacred corpse that had once
been John Murdoch.

"Ask her again," Gino said evenly.

"She's in shock," Quinn explained. "She's not speaking at all."

Murdoch's intestines were strewn across the sand like a pile of
bloody dead eels, his arms stretched out in front of him as if still trying
to ward off whatever had attacked him. His head was turned to the side,
and what had been his good eye was wide open and vacant. A repulsive

combination of blood and bodily fluids he'd vomited coated his chin and neck.

"I said ask her again."

"Give it some time, she—"

"You see what I see, don't you?"

"Of course."

"Then you tell me what could've done this."

Quinn wiped perspiration from her eyes with a shaking hand. "The spinal column's severed so cleanly, it—it could only have been done with a weapon that's incredibly sharp and strong."

"Yeah," Gino said, finally taking his eyes from the carnage long enough to look at her. "Wielded by someone with an incredible amount of strength and skill. I'm talking about precision and power that's almost beyond belief."

Since they'd returned, Herm had spent most of his time pacing back and forth in the sand, muttering to himself. "I told you we weren't alone on this island!" He moved closer. "Did I or did I not tell you we were *not* alone on this fucking island! Whoever did this to Murdoch did the same thing to Andre, and—"

"Ask her again, Quinn," Gino said, ignoring him.

"She's in shock. You've got to give her some time to—"

"We don't have any fucking time!" Standing, he lumbered over to the palm tree Harper had collapsed under. "Hey! Look at me!" Gino grabbed her by the shoulders and shook her. Until that moment Harper

138

hadn't even noticed him, but the force of his grip seemed to snap her back into the present. She looked up at him with an empty stare that looked as if something deep inside her had broken. "Tell me what happened! Who did this to him? Talk, goddamn it! We need to know what happened!"

Quinn ran to them, grabbed Gino by the shoulder and pulled him off her. "Are you out of your mind? Leave her alone!"

Dallas had tried to stay clear of everyone for the last several minutes, but realizing this was no longer possible, hurried over and moved his wife away from Gino, gently taking her around the waist and walking her a few feet back. "Easy."

"We need to know what happened," Gino said, "and we need to know now!"

"Screaming at her isn't going to—"

Harper silenced everyone by slowly raising an arm and pointing at the jungle.

In unison, everyone looked to the area she'd indicated, unsure if something was coming through the jungle toward them or if she was trying to tell them something else.

When nothing appeared, Quinn slipped between Gino and Harper and crouched down in front of her. "Harper, it's me, okay? It's Quinn. Can you tell me what you're pointing at, honey?"

She continued pointing, her eyes larger now and filled with fear, as if she'd suddenly begun to relive what had taken place.

"He came from that direction?" Quinn guessed. "Is that it?"

Harper's eyes shifted and slowly locked on Quinn. She nodded.

"Just one man?"

Her bottom lip quivered as more tears spilled across her cheeks. "There was only one," she said in a tiny voice. "But it didn't look like a man. Not…not exactly."

Despite the heat, a chill throttled Quinn, settling at the back of her neck. "What *did* it look like then?" she asked. "Can you tell me?"

"It came up out of the ground," Harper whispered, as if fearful the killer might hear her. "There." She pointed to the same section of jungle, but more emphatically.

Quinn looked back over her shoulder at the others.

"What the hell does that mean?" Dallas asked, nervously eyeing the jungle. "What does she mean?"

"Harper," Gino said, "baby, what do you mean by it didn't look like a man?"

She kept pointing and staring through her tears at the jungle.

"This isn't happening," Dallas mumbled. "This can't be happening."

Quinn turned back to Harper. "Honey, listen to me. I know you're frightened. We all are. But it's very important that you tell me exactly what you saw, do you understand?"

"It came up out of the ground."

Herm moved toward the jungle, hesitantly approaching the area

140

she'd indicated.

"Get away from there!" Gino called to him. "Stay over here with us, moron."

Without bothering to look in Gino's direction, Herm again flipped him his middle finger and continued studying the edge of the jungle.

"Where were you when it happened?" Quinn asked Harper.

"In the water. I was in the water."

"That's a bit of a distance, are you sure you—"

"It wasn't there and then all of a sudden...it was." She finally lowered her arm. "I saw it come up out of the ground and then...after... it just...disappeared."

"Disappeared how?"

"Back into the ground."

"What was it, Harper? What did you see? What did this?"

While the others watched her, Dallas scanned the jungle, watching for whatever might come charging through at any moment while also trying to keep an eye on Herm and whatever the hell he was up to.

"If it wasn't a man," Quinn asked her, "then what was it?"

"It was like a man," Harper eventually answered. "But it had..."

"Tell me. It's okay. Tell me."

"Horns." She trembled with terror. "And it was covered in like... metal or..."

Quinn glanced at the others with uncertainty.

"It looked like a…"

"Like a what?" Quinn asked, gently rubbing her shoulder.

"Like a monster."

CHAPTER NINE

Gino looked as if he were about to come out of his skin at any moment. His fear and confusion was manifesting as rage, and it was barely contained. "We need to know what's happening," he said through gritted teeth. "Or there's no way to defend ourselves against it. Until we can get her to tell us exactly what she saw, we need to stay put, keep the jungle in front of us and the ocean behind us. It's the only way to see what might be coming at us."

Looking back at the palm tree, where Quinn sat watching the jungle and beneath which Harper had curled into a fetal position, Dallas said, "She's in rough shape, I don't know how much more we're going to get out of her for now." He'd managed to get Gino a short distance from everyone else in an attempt to talk him into a calmer state. Problem was, Dallas was right there with him, teetering precariously on the razor's edge separating sanity from absolute panic and blind terror.

"Yeah, well we need to get that fire a lot bigger and a lot brighter before night falls. Darkness is going to be our enemy now. We can't—I don't—fuck!"

"Look, man, Quinn said it's probably going to be a while before Harper starts making more sense. She says the trauma's been too much for her and—"

"We're all traumatized, Dal. This is bullshit. Weak-ass bullshit we can't afford right now!"

"Not everybody's you. Try to remember that."

"She needs to get over it and put her big girl panties on. This is a life or death situation we're dealing with here! Whatever the fuck's out there cut a grown man in half! In *half*, Dal, you fucking hear me?"

Dallas grabbed him by the arm and pulled him closer, the way a parent might just before disciplining their child. In all the years they'd known each other, he'd never done anything like that, and it stunned them both. "Take a good look at her, Gino. She's a fucking child, and she wasn't exactly splitting the atom before all this. What the hell did you expect? The rest of us are way ahead of her and we're barely holding it together as it is. And we didn't see Murdoch die. You fucking hear *me*?"

This seemed to reach him, as Gino relaxed his posture somewhat, unclenched his fists and pulled his arm free before offering a quick nod. "Yeah, I—it's just—what the hell's happening, man? This is a goddamn nightmare. And now on top of it we got her talking crap about someone popping up out of the ground?"

"It's not crap."

Herm stood a few feet away, scowling at them.

144

"What are you talking about?"

Motioning them to follow, Herm returned to the jungle's edge. As they arrived, Quinn joined them as well.

"When Harper said the killer came up out of the ground," Herm told them, "this is what she was talking about."

A foot or so beyond the edge of the beach, he kicked at some dirt with his sneaker. A whirlpool formed, drawing earth into its spiral before finally ceasing to reveal a ragged opening in the ground roughly the size of a manhole.

"What the hell?" Quinn muttered.

"Best guess, it's part of a tunnel."

"A tunnel? Jesus Christ, what—"

"I don't have all the answers, okay?" Herm explained through a lengthy sigh. "But I can tell you this. The Japanese built tunnels on almost every island they occupied during the Second World War. They were known for their intricate tunnel systems. They used them to move around undetected, but also as a way of literally digging into their positions. Like ticks on a hound. From the looks of the opening it hasn't been used in a long time, which means it was mostly grown over, so when the killer came through it, he had to break and sort of burst right through the earth. From a distance, it would've looked like he appeared out of nowhere and just popped right up out of the ground, because that's exactly what he did."

"After all this time that hole would've been completely grown

145

over," Dallas said. "Wouldn't it be impossible to burst through it like that? That'd take inhuman power."

"You mean like the kind of inhuman power it'd take to cut a grown man in half with a single swing of a weapon, most likely a sword? That kind of power?"

Everyone remained quiet a moment.

"So you're saying these tunnels are all over the island?" Gino asked.

"Without exploring them there's no way to know for sure how extensive they are, but yeah, that's the likeliest scenario. There's probably an entire network of them."

"Okay, wait," Dallas said, hands to his head, "you said the math didn't work, that—"

"It doesn't. There's no way some leftover or forgotten Japanese soldier from that era could be responsible for this," Herm said. "Matter of fact, I'm not sure anything human could cut a man in half like that."

Quinn looked around, as if to be certain they were still alone. "Of course it had to be human. What else would it be?"

"I don't have a fucking clue."

"Gino," Dallas said, "is it possible?"

Still mesmerized by the tunnel opening, he continued staring at it even when he finally answered. "If it was a sword, maybe. It'd have to be incredibly sharp and—I don't know, I—he'd have to be really skilled and so strong, I—"

"Come on, Quinn," Herm interjected, "you're the one with the medical experience. You're telling me even a very strong, very skilled human being, using a very sharp and strong sword, could cut a man Murdoch's size clean in half with a single stroke? Is that what you're expecting us to believe?"

"I'm not expecting anyone to believe anything. But if you want *me* to believe there's some sort of psychopathic supernatural monster—"

"No one said—"

"—running around on this island, I'm going to need a lot more proof."

"Your proof's lying over there in two goddamn pieces."

"Maybe it's someone who was stranded here, like us. Maybe he's gone crazy. Maybe he found the tunnels and uses them, maybe—"

"Maybe that's highly unlikely."

"As unlikely as a *supernatural* explanation? Seriously?"

"My point is—"

"It doesn't matter," Gino said suddenly. He'd finally taken his attention from the tunnel. "None of it."

"What's that supposed to mean?"

"It means I don't give a fuck if it's the Easter Bunny. Whoever—*what*ever—it is, it's already killed two of us, and it's only a matter of time before it comes looking for the rest of us." Gino gazed out at the jungle. "So for now, we cover this hole as best we can and keep a close eye on it, we arm ourselves with whatever we can lay our hands on, we get that fire blazing big and bright as possible, and we ride the night out here on the beach."

"And then?"

"First light, we go back to the other side of the island and set ourselves up in a better, more easily defendable position, maybe in one the buildings. It's a smaller area, so there's not as much we have to keep an eye on. From there we figure out what the hell it is we're dealing with here. That camp holds the answers. It has to."

No one spoke again for what seemed an eternity.

The island and the ocean whispered to them, filling the silence.

"What about Murdoch?" Herm asked.

Gino turned and walked away. "Bury him."

As the daylight hours wound down, the fear only increased. In solemn and workmanlike silence, Dallas and Quinn buried Murdoch's remains not far from where they'd entombed Natalie, making sure to keep an eye on the jungle as they did so. Upon moving the body to the hole they'd dug, Dallas stopped and retched violently. Just dry heaves, he was unable to bring up anything, but it took a horrible toll on him physically, leaving his gut aching and his throat sore. In all the years they'd been together, this was something beyond anything he or Quinn could have imagined, much less thought they'd find themselves doing. But at least she'd seen her share of dead bodies and carnage in the past, Dallas had never witnessed anything like what had happened to Murdoch, and it left him rattled and deeply disturbed in ways he never realized were possible. One moment Murdoch was a living, breathing human being. The next he was mangled, split into two halves, a *thing* that had been butchered. Despite the horror of it all, it refused to compute in Dallas's mind, so with robotic motion, he did what needed to be done, and for the time being, left his mind the flat-line of shock it had become.

"You okay?" Quinn asked.

Dallas responded with a sideways glance as he continued moving sand and dirt.

"I know it's a ridiculous question at this point," she admitted. "But it's all I've got."

"I know it's just beginning, but I want this to be over. I'm not cut out for this shit, Quinn. I'm a schoolteacher, for Christ's sake."

"Nobody's cut out for this."

"I'm not even sure what *this* is anymore."

"It's a fight. It has been since that boat went down and we went into the water."

"And now the world's gone insane, and us along with it. Nothing makes sense anymore." He crawled closer to her, struggling to control his emotions. "Never been so goddamned frightened in all my life."

"Me either," Quinn said softly. "If I thought I could get away with it, I'd curl up in a ball and have myself a good cry. Then I'd go to sleep, and when I woke up we'd be back home. Safe and sound."

His eyes filled with tears. "I'm sorry."

"You have nothing to be sorry about."

"I need to be stronger."

"You're plenty strong." She reached out and touched his wrist, holding it a while and stroking it gently with her thumb. "You're one of the strongest people I've ever known, and I love you. More than anything in the world."

A spasm-like smile twitched across his face as he cupped her face with his hand. "Love you too."

She leaned in closer and they kissed.

"Let's finish this," Quinn said.

While they did, Herm continued tending to the fire. He had it going good and strong, while acting as a sentry of sorts, watching the jungle and the tunnel opening as best he could.

Gino and Harper had ventured farther down the beach to the rocks and caves in search of food. Even though Herm and Quinn had done the same earlier and come up virtually empty, after an hour or so, Gino returned with a decent-sized crab. Still alive but skewered on one of the makeshift spears he'd made, the creature's legs moved and clicked like an alien entity while Harper looked on in disgust.

"Holy cow, will you look at that," Herm said, noticing the crab. "Where'd you find that sucker?"

Rather than answer, Gino looked over at the flames. "Good job on the fire."

Genuinely surprised, it took Herm a moment to reply. "Thanks."

"Keep feeding it. I want it big as we can get it tonight."

"It's not like whatever's out there doesn't know we're here."

"Good chance it's watching us right now." Gino looked to the jungle. "Obviously whatever it is has no issue attacking in broad daylight, but in the dark we'll be at an even bigger disadvantage. That's why I want this beach lit up like a stadium. If it tries to hit us tonight, I want to see the sonofabitch coming."

Herm eyed the crab as it struggled, impaled on the stick. His mouth watering, he could already taste the meat inside that shell. "God, I'm so hungry."

"Well, tonight we eat."

"Looking forward to it, trust me, but we need to get a hold of some weapons too," Herm said, forcing his mind away from the food. "I don't know what we're dealing with yet, but whatever it is, something tells me a bunch of pointy sticks aren't going to cut it."

"I know. I'm working on it. For now, stay alert."

Herm nodded and gave a smile. This was the first civil conversation he and Gino had engaged in since before they'd left the resort. Even on the yacht Gino had been aloof and short with him, and though he knew they would never—*could* never—be friends, it was nice to take even a brief respite from the constant bickering.

Without a word, Harper shuffled over to the fire and sat down before it, staring into the flames and shooting sparks as if in a trance.

"She all right?" Herm asked quietly.

Gino glanced at her then returned his focus to the jungle. "No."

"Keep waiting for the other shoe to drop. Every time I hear a noise or look at the jungle I expect something to come running out at us, I'm a goddamn bundle of nerves. I can't imagine what it must've been like for her to actually see it happen." Herm scratched at the back of his neck. "I wish I hadn't said those things to Murdoch. I didn't—I mean—I didn't even get a chance to make it right with him, I—I don't always mean the things I say, I—I need to learn to keep quiet sometimes, I—"

"Much as I'm all for you shutting the hell up more often, an old salt like Murdoch should've known better and gotten us the hell out of there well ahead of that storm. Truth of it is he was in his cabin drinking and leaving everything to Davis when he should've been on top of things. Cost Davis his life and almost killed the rest of us in the process. So for whatever it's worth coming from me," Gino said, moving by him and toward the fire, "you were right. Fuck him."

Unsure which had stunned him more—Gino's attempt at kindness or his final remark—Herm struggled to decide how, or even if, he should react. He was saved by Dallas and Quinn, who returned to camp just then, dirty and bathed in sweat.

"It's done," Dallas told him.

Herm motioned to Gino, who was kneeling by the fire with the crab. "Our illustrious leader caught us dinner."

"Oh my God," Quinn said, hurrying toward him. "Food!"

Dallas was starving too, but his stomach was still sore from the heaving. Part of him wanted to embrace the exhaustion and desire to simply shut down, but the island had become too dangerous for that now. Instead, he held tight to the growing cold anger building inside him, the base side he'd always rejected, the primal slithering up out of the darkest parts of his psyche like a warrior summoned to battle.

Out over the ocean, clouds crept in, slowly stealing the sun.

"Here comes the night," Herm said.

Already blood on the sun, Dallas thought. *Why not the moon?*

Gino killed the crab as, one-by-one, they converged on it, tearing the creature apart and ripping free the meat, stabbing it with their sticks and pushing it into the fire in a frenzy of hunger, lust, fear and anguish.

Concealed within the jungle, but closer than they could've imagined, something watched with a hunger and bloodlust all its own.

CHAPTER TEN

Fire cut the night, crackling and spitting sparks and flame into the air the more they fed it, the stronger it grew, the harder it fought the darkness. Primeval and hypnotic, it possessed power and magic unlike anything else, and on the beach, it provided enough light to illuminate their camp and a sizeable surrounding area. Despite their exhaustion, sleep came only in short, fitful intervals, if at all. Still crippled with terror, Harper spent hours gazing blankly into the fire or watching the darkness and jungle beyond. Quinn tried to talk with her a few times in the hopes of assessing and getting a better handle on her emotional and mental state, but Harper was either uninterested or unable to engage, and mostly ignored her.

While Herm fed the fire, Gino roamed about like a restless ghost, walking the sand or moving about down near the water before disappearing into the night, only to return moments later. On one of his rounds, he noticed Dallas had left Quinn by the fire and was walking the sand between their camp and the ocean. It reminded Gino of better times, though he wasn't sure why. He'd never seen his friend so worn out, so depleted and frightened, so weary. Yet in that strange moment, where only the vaguest of shadows revealed his presence, Gino remembered the happier times they'd shared.

We'll never know that again. Even if we beat the odds and get off this godforsaken island, even if we somehow make it home, we'll never know that kind of peace and abandon again. This will always be with us, a scar that will never heal.

In that awful darkness, as the night slogged on, Gino thought about his life and all the things he'd done. So much wasted time, he realized now. Sure, he'd been on countless adventures, seen and been to places most only read about and experienced things most only watched on television. But beyond that, what had he really done with his life? Dallas and Quinn had each other. They'd built a life together and were as much in love as they'd been the day they were married and he'd served as Dallas's best man. He had Harper, but he didn't even know her that well. Truth was, he'd never cared to. She was tits, ass and a pretty face, a distraction, someone there to help him feel younger than he was and to keep his ego inflated. He fucked her because he could, not because he had any real feelings for her. Now, in the dark of night so far from home, Gino knew he'd let the really important things slip free. It had been a trade, he knew, and one he'd always felt was worth it. He was free, no responsibilities beyond his job, and could come and go as he pleased, do the things he wanted to do, buy the things he wanted to buy, enjoy his life as he saw fit however he saw fit whenever he saw fit. So why did he feel so unfulfilled, so unhappy, especially now that he realized he might never get a chance to make it all right? Because he'd been wrong, and he knew that now. Maybe just like Harper he was nothing but a distraction too, a mild amusement for others, the rugged outdoorsy tough guy with the vacuous good-looks and the body most guys half his age would've killed for, a cliché others rolled their eyes over and laughed at when he wasn't looking.

The voice deep within him continued to whisper things he didn't want to hear, and though he made a conscious effort, he was unable to silence it. Perhaps it was just his own voice rattling around in his head, but Gino couldn't be sure. Perhaps it was a premonition, an instinctual warning designed to let him know their days were numbered and now was the time to acknowledge these things, before it was too late to atone for them. Even if he only did so in his mind, maybe that might buy him peace, knowing that if he had the chance again, he'd do things right. He'd look for love, not just sex, and try to build a life about something other than his wants and desires. He thought of his parents, his sisters and their children—his nieces and nephews—his other friends back home, the guys at work, and how he'd let them all down by rarely being there for them or focusing on anything but himself.

Or maybe that was just more pie-in-the-sky bullshit. Maybe none of it made a goddamn bit of difference because none of them would ever leave this place alive. There was a predator on this island, and they were its prey. Like any animal, Man knew when Death was near. Maybe his years of working out and preparation would turn out to be more than vanity after all, Gino thought. Here, in this hell, it was an asset, a weapon, and one they desperately needed.

Maybe it was here that he'd make a difference in not just his own life, but the lives of others as well, of these people who counted on him. Gino had never been the religious sort, and when it came to spiritual matters, considered himself an agnostic. But if there *was* greater purpose to this life, if things did, in fact, happen for a reason, as so many people often said and seemed to believe, maybe this was what it had all led up to. Maybe he'd been training and working for this his entire life without ever realizing it.

Gino glared defiantly at the night, the jungle, as if willing his fear away and transferring it to the darkness and whatever hid within it.

This is my shot, he thought.

"I'm coming out of my skin."

Startled and immediately upset with himself for letting his guard down even for a moment, he saw that Dallas had sidled up next to him. "Few more hours," he said, feigning a casual tone, "it'll be light."

"Murdoch was killed in broad daylight." Dallas scratched at the growth of beard along his chin. "We're not safe either way."

"Neither is whatever's out there." From the corner of his eye, Gino saw Dallas nod, but he wasn't sure he believed him this time.

"Look, if something happens to me, I want you to promise you'll—"

158

"Nothing's going to happen to you, Dal."

"If it does…"

Gino finally looked at him.

"You make sure Quinn—"

"You kidding? Quinn's the toughest one here."

"You know what I mean."

"I'll die before I let anything happen to her," Gino told him. "Or you."

"Me too." Dallas cleared his throat awkwardly. "I need to ask you something, and I want you to be honest with me."

"Have I lied to you yet?"

"Far as I know, not in all the years I've known you."

"Then ask."

"Can we get off the island? Can you build something that we can survive on out there? Is it possible?"

"Possible? Yeah, sure, it's possible."

"But not likely?"

"It's not like the movies, where you go into the jungle and with no problem find all the right things and all of sudden you have a seaworthy raft. If we can do it, and I mean *if*, we're talking about a lot of work, even more luck, and we'll need the right materials and tools. *Real* tools, not a bunch of sharpened sticks. Hopefully once we scavenge that outpost we can find what we need, but even if we do, our chances on the open ocean aren't good either, Dal."

"Believe me, I'm in no hurry to go back out there, but we don't have much choice. We can't stay here, man. We need to run."

"Never been much of a runner."

"Neither have I, but we need to get the hell off this island, because whatever's out there, we're not equipped to fight it. You saw what was left of Andre. You saw what it did to Murdoch. We can't fight this thing. We *can't*."

Gino's dark eyes slowly panned through the darkness. "We may have to."

"We'll die."

"Better to die swinging than running."

"Christ, it almost sounds like you *want* to fight it."

"I want to live."

"I want everyone to live."

Gino took a step away, farther from the fire and deeper into the night. "Keep an eye on things, I'm gonna make another sweep. Be back in a few."

Dallas looked to the fire. "Maybe I should go with you this time," he said.

But Gino was already gone.

GREG F. GIFUNE

By the time the sun had risen high in the sky, bringing with it the usual stifling heat that draped the island, they had returned to the outpost with what little they had. There wasn't much drinkable water left, but Gino was able to rig a section of the rubber raft they'd originally used as a rain-catcher into a makeshift canteen of sorts. By tying off the end with a strong thin vine, it formed a pouch of liquid that could be more easily transported without spilling. They made torches and carried the fire with them, leaving the bonfire they'd spent all night feeding to burn down on the far beach.

Now, in the shadows of the outpost, they stood watching the buildings and listening to the jungle surrounding them. They'd been certain an attack would occur between camp and the outpost, but none came. The resulting stress and tension, the horrible anticipation, was crippling.

"Why doesn't it attack us?" Quinn asked, scanning the section of jungle from which they'd come. "What's it waiting for?"

"Maybe it's toying with us," Herm suggested. "You know, like a cat does with a mouse? When I was a kid, I had this cat, Ruffles, and whenever he caught a mouse he'd let it almost get away, you know? But right before it got to the end of his reach, he'd pluck it up and pull it back over to him. He'd do that for hours sometimes, and every time that poor mouse would make a break for it, thinking it was going to get away. The whole thing seemed to amuse Ruffles, but when he finally tired of it, he'd kill the fucker. Quickly. Efficiently. Then he'd eat it."

161

"That was comforting," Dallas said. "Great story."

"I loved that cat. He was my best friend when I was a kid."

"A predator always has the advantage of knowing when and where and how it's going to attack," Gino said, finally weighing in. "What we need to do is establish a defendable position here. Then we'll use the torches and search the main building, see what we can find."

"Which building are we bunking in?" Herm asked.

"None just yet." Gino motioned to the nearby beach and lagoon. "We need to set up camp there for now. Small area, only one way in or out. If anything comes at us—"

"When."

It was the first thing Harper had said in hours, and silenced Gino in midsentence.

"It's coming back for us," she continued, her cartoonish voice void of any emotion whatsoever, "and there's nothing we can do about it."

"We'll not only be able to see something coming," Gino said through a hard sigh, "we'll have a better chance of defending ourselves and our position. Once things are under control, or if the elements get bad again, we can always take shelter in one of these buildings. But until we know what's going on and what we're dealing with, we need a more secure position, and the lagoon is it. Now let's get to work."

With that, they set to performing as best they could what had become their rituals. They set up camp on the small stretch of beach before the lagoon. Herm handled getting the fire going, using the torches to light up the driftwood and other small burnable sticks and vegetation the others had gathered. Once it was underway, Gino secured the water and few supplies they had while Dallas rummaged and found numerous metal containers he washed out in the lagoon and positioned about as rain catchers. Quinn took charge of the torches, making certain both kept burning.

And then, with Herm in possession of one torch and Quinn the other, the group moved as one, like displaced children lost in a nightmare, back along the sandy path to the outpost. They stopped before the formidable building. The heavy metal door, ajar like they'd left it, awaited them.

"Shouldn't someone stay behind and keep an eye out?" Herm asked.

"We stay together," Gino said, reaching for a thick, club-like piece of wood partially concealed in the dirt at his feet. "If it wasn't so heavy we could close the door behind us and secure it, but I'm worried we might not be able to get it back open, so we'll just have to risk it and stay alert. From now on, we stay together."

"Gino," Quinn said, "what if it's already in there?"

He wrenched the club free of the ground and inspected it, testing the weight of it against his other hand, slapping it down into his open palm. Satisfied, he approached the door, then looked back at the others. "That's a chance we'll have to take."

"But—"

"Strength in numbers," Dallas said before further argument could ensue. "Right?"

Quinn brushed a strand of sweaty hair from her forehead. "Let's hope so."

"Herm," Gino said, "take point."

Rather than responding with one of his typical wisecracks, Herm dutifully headed through the opening, letting his torch light the way ahead.

Harper latched onto Gino's arm, clinging to it with both hands. Gently as he could, he loosened her grip, and instead, took her by the hand and led her through the partially open doorway. Dallas and Quinn pulled up the rear, so one torch led the way into the darkness and the other lit an area behind them.

Moving gradually but decisively, Herm swept the torch back and forth in slow deliberate arcs, illuminating as large an area as possible. "What the hell's all over the floor?" He came to an abrupt stop and held the torch down by his leg. "Something's crunching under my feet with every step."

"I thought it was sand," Dallas said.

"No, look."

A large amount of the substance lined an area in front of the doorway and continued a few feet into the room. It looked a bit like sand but the color was wrong and the grains were larger, thicker than sand.

"Is that *salt*?"

"Yeah, I think it is." Gino pressed a thumb into it and hesitantly brought it to his mouth. Touching it with the tip of his tongue, he looked to the others and nodded.

"Why would there be so much salt all over the floor?" Dallas asked.

"Spillage?"

"No, the pattern is too deliberate."

"Maybe a religious thing," Quinn offered.

"Salt is used in a lot of Japanese magic and religious rituals." Herm moved the torchlight slowly along the floor. "It's usually used to cleanse an area of evil spirits or that kind of thing, far as I know. When it's around doorways or windows, it's usually for preventing evil to enter or exit an area, I think."

Quinn looked away and raised her torch higher, broadening the light around them. "Because this place wasn't already creepy enough."

"My best guess is they performed some sort of ritual here." Herm reached for a small brocade bag resting atop the salt. Inside, he found a thin rectangular piece of wood covered in red silk. The sides on one end of the wood were slanted rather than squared off, and attached to the silk were several small pieces of paper bearing Japanese characters. "Pretty sure this is a talisman designed to ward off evil, or for protection, that kind of thing. I don't remember the term for these things, but they're a fairly standard item in Shinto and Buddhism. These little papers are probably prayers or incantations of some sort."

"I don't want to be in here," Harper whined, attaching herself to Gino again.

"Easy." He wrapped an arm around her. "I got you."

"Whatever was going on," Herm said, standing, "they were worried about it enough that they tried to purify the area on the way out."

"I don't think it worked," Quinn said. "*Purified* isn't exactly the vibe I'm getting from this place."

Herm aimed his torch at the darkness ahead. The flame revealed countless scraps of paper and other office supplies littering the floor beyond the carpet of salt, as well as several pieces of furniture—mostly chairs, small tables and file drawers—scattered about. A large drum of some kind, possibly for gasoline, lay on its side directly in their path. "Careful." He pointed it out, led everyone around it, then crouched down again and scooped up a handful of papers from the floor. "Looks like mostly forms and parts of reports," he said, shining his torch on them for a better look. "From the markings it's definitely official military paperwork of some kind, but I don't have clue what any of it says."

Quinn used her torch to cast light on the walls. Though pitted and worn, thus far, they were the same as the rest of the building and most of its contents—remarkably well-preserved. Unlike most of the outpost, the island had not reclaimed this place, and it had been sealed shut for so long, it was as if time had simply stopped within these walls, preserving things nearly as the Japanese forces had left them.

The air was thinner here, and it was far cooler than outside, but an unpleasant odor hung around them like a fog. A slowly tightening noose, the claustrophobic feel to the low ceilings and dense walls, the surrounding darkness and the ghosts that surely watched them from the shadows across all those years, grew stronger and more oppressive the deeper into the building they went.

Quinn's torch settled on a large rising sun flag on the far wall, the colors faded. As the light continued along the wall, it revealed shelves still stocked with various items, mostly bottles and small boxes. Although covered in a thick film of dust, everything appeared to be intact. She moved closer, carefully chose a bottle from one of the shelves, blew the dust off of it and tried to get a closer look at the label. Replacing it to the shelf, she looked over a few other items then turned to the others. "These are medical supplies."

"Was this a hospital?" Gino asked.

"There's no way they'd have a hospital this size at an island outpost," Herm answered for her. "Maybe this part of it was used as a sickbay kind of thing, though."

"Keep moving." Gino, still holding Harper's hand, motioned for Herm to continue.

Herm dropped the papers and pushed his torch into the darkness awaiting them.

Shadows slid along the walls, dust motes spiraled in the torchlight, and all the sounds from the ocean and jungle they'd grown accustomed to could no longer be heard this deep into the building. Other than their breath and footfalls, it was deathly quiet. Once inside these old walls, the outside world ceased to exist in any meaningful way.

They moved through an open doorway, the door itself resting on the floor a few feet away, badly damaged and looking as if it had been forcibly removed from its hinges then tossed aside.

Once into the next room, they encountered a series of tables, chairs, small cabinets and metal counters. As Herm lowered the torch toward the only table still standing upright, the light fell upon a pair of leather shackles. Built directly into the table, there were two sets, one for hands and another for feet.

"You guys seeing this?"

"Okay, this was definitely some sort of medical building," Quinn said. "But..."

"What's with the restraints?" Dallas asked.

Quinn held her torch lower, sweeping it to illuminate the floor. Like the others before it, it was covered in papers and debris. But here, there was something more.

Photographs.

She bent down and picked one up, and then another and another.

Black-and-white, grainy and badly faded with age, they were otherwise undamaged. The first several revealed the room they were now standing in, and a shot of a man shackled to one of the beds. In the photographs, a clearly crazed and sickly looking young Japanese soldier was strapped down but struggling to free himself, a look of abject terror on his pale face, his mouth open wide and twisted, the camera having evidently captured him in mid-scream. In the final photograph, blood smears emanating from the man's eyes stained his cheeks in wide swaths, his abdomen was split and held open with some sort of metal contraption, his intestines in full view across his lap and along the table. Attached to the photograph was a single sheet report of some kind.

"Jesus," Quinn said softly, handing them over so the others could see them too.

Gino squinted at them through the poor lighting. "What the hell is this?"

"I don't know."

Dallas studied the photographs once Gino had passed them to him. "What in God's name were they doing out here?"

"Whatever it was," Herm said, looking over his shoulder at them, "I don't think it had anything to do with God."

"Torture?"

"Possibly." As the photos were returned to her Quinn dropped them back to the floor, no longer wanting to touch them. "Or medical experiments, maybe, I don't know."

"People think of the Nazis when it comes to human experimentation," Herm said, "but the Japanese were involved in that shit too. It was called Unit 731. Hideous stuff. We're talking chemical and biological warfare, vivisections, rape and forced pregnancy, depriving people of food, water and sleep, injecting them with all sorts of diseases and other poisons, syphilis, anthrax, bubonic plague, cholera, the whole—"

"I think we get it," Quinn said.

"There were rumored to be occult ties to certain factions too."

"Occult?"

"Experiments that supposedly yielded results, contact with unknown entities and other realities, that kind of thing. The Nazis reported similar things."

"Sounds like folklore to me."

"Could be. Who knows?"

"And the Japanese did these experiments on their own people?" Dallas asked.

"Mostly Chinese and Koreans, prisoners of war, but in some cases, yeah, they even experimented on their own soldiers. A lot of women and children were used too. We're talking about evil on an almost unimaginable level."

"I've never heard any of this. Were the people involved tried for war crimes?"

"The Russians tried a few, if I remember correctly."

"What about us?" Dallas pressed.

"We gave them immunity in exchange for their results and data.

Under the American occupation, members of Unit 731 walked free."

"Unbelievable," Gino said.

Quinn rubbed her temples with her free hand. "My God."

"Yeah." Herm looked around and wearily shook his head. "Thing is I don't remember anything about island outposts being used. Most of these things took place in facilities in Japan. I mean, look, I'm reciting what I remember from college a million years ago and some of my own research, okay? I'm not an expert on this by any stretch of the imagination."

"Could this have been some sort of satellite program?" Quinn asked.

"It's possible, an offshoot, maybe. Let's face it, if you were doing things you never wanted anyone to know about, this'd be a great place to do it."

No one spoke for a while, and the eerie silence returned, engulfing them.

"All right," Gino finally said, "let's keep moving."

Herm swept his torch back and forth along the floor and walls, revealing another doorway leading to a dark corridor beyond. With a quick fearful look over his shoulder at the others, he turned and led them through the room and into the hallway.

Narrow and confining, they had to fall into single-file in order to negotiate the corridor. Above them, old light fixtures encased in metal cages lined the ceiling, the walls and floors bare. Like a tomb, it engulfed them, and even with the light from the torches, the darkness seemed different here, deeper and more menacing.

The first side room they came to was small and cramped, with a bank of electronics and communications equipment along the walls. Old and covered in dust and cobwebs, the equipment had been purposely smashed and broken apart. On the floor just inside the doorway they found the likely culprit, a large metal ax.

Tossing his club aside, Gino retrieved the ax and inspected it.

"They destroyed all their communications and radio equipment," Dallas said. "Why would they do that?"

"It's not that unusual, actually," Herm explained. "It's a fairly common practice in wartime when abandoning this sort of equipment."

"This is a game changer." Gino smiled broadly, holding up the ax as if in evidence. "It's almost like new. Not only a good weapon, but one hell of a tool. It's gonna make things a lot easier."

Quinn's torch found an overturned chair near the corner, likely something the radio operator had used. But as she moved closer, focusing the flame on the floor around it, she noticed something more.

"Christ, that's *blood*," Dallas said.

An enormous dark blood stain covered most of the chair and the cement floor surrounding it. A good deal of spatter lined not only the nearest wall, but had sprayed across the ceiling as well. Long absorbed into the walls and floor, the stain had turned dark over time, but the sheer size of it was shocking.

172

"I don't want to be in here," Harper said again. "I want to leave."

Ignoring her, they all moved back into the corridor and continued on, deeper into the building. Harper never left Gino's side, still holding his hand tight.

The flames licked the walls, flickering through the shadows and darkness, but the corridor seemed more claustrophobic and confining than ever. The floor was littered with more papers, but something in particular stood out. Herm bent down and picked it up.

"What the hell?"

"What's wrong? What is it?"

He held up a tattered and faded magazine. A young Katherine Hepburn graced the cover, which was dated January 6, 1941 and had a price of ten cents. "A copy of LIFE Magazine," Herm said.

Gino raised an eyebrow. "Why would there be an American magazine *here*?"

"No idea. Strange."

"Could American forces have been here at some point too?" Dallas asked.

"Seems doubtful. I mean, there's nothing else I've seen that would indicate that, but…"

"But?"

"Well, like Gino said, why would this be here? There were no Americans on the island, not even POWs from what we've seen. And even if there were, where the hell would a copy of LIFE Magazine with

Katherine Hepburn on the cover have come from?"

"Who's Katherine Hepburn?" Harper asked quietly.

But for a quick sideways glance from Herm, they ignored her.

"Maybe it had something to do with one of the experiments," Dallas said.

"Possible, I guess."

"Can I see it?" Quinn asked.

Herm handed it to her.

She stared at it. Had she seen this magazine before somewhere?

Dallas sensed her discomfort. "What's wrong?"

"I don't know. I..." Had she dreamed of this?

"It's definitely out of place," Herm said through a heavy sigh. "Makes no sense."

"You're right. It doesn't." Quinn tossed it back to the floor. "Let's keep moving."

They followed the corridor for several more feet. Eventually, it led to another room, this one the largest of any they'd encountered thus far.

"Okay," Herm said just above a whisper. "We've got bodies."

The skeletal remains of two Japanese soldiers lay on the floor just inside the doorway, one with a rifle by his side and a gasmask still covering his face, the other clutching a gasmask in one hand and a rifle in the other. The gasmasks, made of rubber and covered in some sort of mesh fabric, had oversized goggle-like eye pieces, giving the long dead

174

soldier a disturbingly alien and frightening appearance.

"Gasmasks," Dallas muttered. "That can't be good."

"We shouldn't be in here," Harper said in her tiny voice.

Quinn angled her torch deeper into the room. Several human skulls and bones, some still inside uniforms, others not, lay scattered about, along with more paperwork, cans, boxes and additional photographs. As the light crept across the room, it stopped on one skull in particular. There were still strands of hair stuck to it.

Alongside it lay a machete.

Dallas scooped it up. It was heavy and filthy, but intact. He held it up to show the others.

"Nice," Gino said. "Now we're getting somewhere."

Herm took another step, realized he was standing on something, and held the torch down so he could get a better look. Dog tags on a chain lay beneath one of his sneakers. "There must be—what—six or seven bodies in here?"

As she slowly swept her torch through the room, Quinn stopped briefly on a bank of file cabinets that lined the back wall, then another examination table in the corner. There appeared to be something on it, so she moved closer.

A hideously decayed face pierced the darkness, as if it had lurched out at her.

"Jesus!" she said, stumbling back.

Herm replaced her light with his. The body lay face-up on the table, head turned to the side and facing them, legs still in restraints. Partially mummified and clad in what remained of a tattered and bloody uniform, the body appeared to have been a young man who, if his open mouth was any indication, had died screaming. His hands were buried in his abdomen up to the wrists.

"This man tore into his own stomach," Quinn said softly. "Imagine the things you'd have to do to someone to make them rip their own guts out."

Dallas picked up some photographs at his feet, and standing close to Quinn so he could benefit from the light from her torch, rifled through them, tossing them back to the floor as he moved from one to the next. Each depicted various test subjects on the beds, and many looked to have been tortured and mutilated to a point where they were barely recognizable as human. Some had been outfitted with strange metal faceplates that appeared to have been drilled or screwed directly into their skulls, while others had something resembling a metal horse bit fastened to their mouths and jaws. Others still looked as if they'd had their eyes removed and had been skinned alive. "Most of these guys look like they're still kids," he said, gagging. "Late teens, early twenties at most. They look…Christ, they look…"

"Possessed," Gino said, looking over Dallas's shoulder at the last photograph in his hand. "They look fucking possessed, like something out of the goddamn Exorcist. Look at his face, his eyes, or what's left of them."

176

"Extreme pain does strange things to people."

Gino turned to Herm. "What was this occult shit you were talking about before they were supposedly doing?"

"I don't—I'm not an—I don't know the specifics, really." He ran the back of his free hand across his mouth and drew a deep breath. "The whole Unit 731 thing is something I cover in my class when we're on World War II. But it's like three minutes, basic, general stuff. I told you, I'm not an expert on this. All I know is from some of the things I've read there were offshoots of the program that dealt with the occult."

"Dealt with it how?"

"Tying black arts and whatnot into the tests they were performing."

"Why? Why would they do that?"

"I don't know."

"What were they trying to achieve?"

"Gino, I promise you, I have no fucking idea."

"Give me your best guess."

Herm thought about it a while. "Well, as for the Japanese specifically, I know their culture is steeped in the spiritual world. Ghosts, for example, play a huge part in their history and culture even to this day. I think they likely would've incorporated magic or rituals they were familiar with culturally—which accounts for the salt and talisman—but at the end of the day, seems like the point was to tap into whatever lies beyond our reality and utilize it for their own purposes. First and foremost, governments always try to figure out how something can be weaponized or used for power and control. Why would anything they may have come across in the world of the occult be any different?"

"Maybe because the world of the occult doesn't exist?" Quinn scoffed.

Gino glanced at her dismissively. "Herm, you said something about entities. What was that shit all about?"

"Supposedly the Japanese introduced black magic and dark rituals into these occult programs to try and see into other realms. You know, the afterlife, other dimensions, the spirit world, that kind of thing. I didn't take it that seriously, to be honest. I assumed it was something that happened because they'd broken these people's minds during the tests and torture. Our government did something similar with the MK-Ultra Project. All sorts of depravation tests were done, there was horrible physical, sexual and psychological abuse, and in a lot of those cases, once the subjects' minds were shattered they started to see shit too."

"Entities and other realities?" Gino asked. "Like these motherfuckers?"

Herm shrugged helplessly. "I—yeah—I guess so."

"Was it real? Did it actually happen?"

"Of course not," Quinn interrupted. "The poor souls were hallucinating."

"Problem is, if they *were* hallucinating," Herm said, "somehow they all saw the same things."

"They likely saw *similar* things," Quinn countered, "not identical."

"The man asked what I knew, Quinn. I'm doing my best to answer him, all right? According to what little I've read on this, the reports claimed the test subjects saw the same entities, the same realms. Not similar, the same. Maybe that's bullshit, but—"

"*Maybe*? Seriously?"

"I don't know," Gino said. "This shit looks pretty real to me."

Quinn pushed by them, heading back toward the corridor. "The death, torture and horrors that took place here were obviously very real. But it was human beings that did these things. There's no such thing as spirits or demons. God forgive them for what they did here, but the only monsters in this world are human."

"In *this* world," Dallas said.

"Yeah, Dal, in this world. You know, the one we're in."

"What about whatever's out there?"

Quinn stopped in the doorway and looked back. Her eyes found her husband in the darkness. "What about it?"

"Maybe it's..."

"Whatever's on this island with us is as human as we are. It has to be."

Harper's eyes filled with tears. "But it's not," she said, trembling.

Rather than respond, Quinn turned and slipped into the corridor.

The others followed, leaving the room, and all its carnage to the dark.

Where it belonged.

CHAPTER ELEVEN

They stood by the firelight, staring at the iron contraptions before them.

"Depravation chambers," Quinn said.

Most were large enough to easily accommodate a grown man, but a couple were smaller, and designed for the subject to be forced into a fetal position before the lid was closed and locked behind them. All but two were outfitted with a round window in the front roughly the size of a saucer. On the opposite wall was a long table and some overturned chairs, which had once most likely served as some sort of observation and reporting area. In one of the chairs still upright, a body sat crumpled over, clad in what was left of a tattered lab coat, head resting on the table, skeletal arms dangling, fingers of bone frozen in a reach for the floor. Closer inspection revealed a pistol near his feet, and a large hole blown out through the back of the man's skull. Whatever had happened here, he'd chosen to put a gun in his mouth and pull the trigger rather than face it.

Three more skeletons lay on the floor near the depravation tanks. All three had been executed, shot in the head while kneeling. Two were without clothing, hands bound with wire at the wrist and fastened behind their backs.

The third wore a uniform, but it was different than the others they'd seen.

Kicking a pair of old helmets and other debris out of the way, Herm crouched down next to the body and studied the markings and patches on the clothing. "This one was Australian," he said. "Good chance these others were too. Must've been POWs."

Along the other wall, Quinn found a series of shelves holding an array of jars and other items. But it wasn't until she held the torch closer that she realized the things in the jars were human body parts and internal organs floating in murky fluid. She forced a swallow and backed away, but the others had seen it too.

"My God," she said in a loud whisper. "What is wrong with us?"

"Don't lump us in with this fucking scum," Gino scoffed, turning toward her with one of his typical confrontational poses. "I've never done anything like this, have you? Would you? *Could* you?"

Quinn never gave him an answer, but not because she didn't have one.

"Hey, through here," Herm said, noticing a door that led to another room. An old ring of keys still hung from the lock, but the door was open, so he ventured inside.

182

The others followed.

A small and boxy area, a row of three concrete cells lined the back wall.

A closer look revealed the thick wood doors on each cell had been outfitted with a small slot one could look through, but due to the lack of light, it was impossible to make out anything.

Herm tried the first door. Locked.

The second was unlocked, but except for a wooden pallet in the corner that looked to have been some sort of primitive bed, it was empty.

Herm moved to the third door. It too was unlocked, but as he stepped inside, allowing the torch to illuminate the cell around him, the walls came to life. Completely covered with an eerie series of scrawls and writing scratched into the concrete itself, it looked like what it probably was, the scribblings of a madman.

"Holy shit," Herm mumbled.

A skeleton sat slumped over in one corner. The cell contained the same sort of pallet bed the previous one had, but this one had been torn apart. The planks lay in a pile, nails protruding from many of them. Herm swept the torch back over to the body. A nail was still clutched in the prisoner's skeletal hand.

"These torches aren't going to last much longer," Quinn said from somewhere behind him. "We need to…"

Her voice fell silent when she saw the walls, and then the body.

Herm had already begun reading what he could. "He was

Australian, an officer, a POW they transported here with a bunch of others. His name and rank are here. He…"

Much of what was there was difficult to read, partly because much of it had faded, partly because the writing was scratched and done in an obviously weak and shaky hand, and partly because the man had been put in this cell and starved to death while being monitored and studied.

"He was trying to tell his story here," Herm said through a hard swallow. "They put him in here and just watched him die. Slowly, over time. No food or water. It's hard to follow but he was trying to tell what happened here, the things they were doing."

"Why would they let him write that on the walls?" Dallas asked.

"Not sure. Maybe seeing what he'd do and what he was thinking was part of the experiment."

"But why would they leave it there? I mean, if this whole thing was so secretive, why allow a prisoner to leave behind evidence and explanations of what was going on?"

"Because this guy wasn't going anywhere," Gino said. "He was gonna die in that cell and nobody was ever gonna come for him or even find this place, so who cares what the poor bastard scratches into the walls?"

Herm ran his free hand over his face then continued to read where he could make out the words. After several minutes, he continued to relay what he could to the others. "He knew he was dying, he…he

184

says goodbye to his parents and his sister, he—it's hard to make out everything—he...he keeps writing he's in Hell." He continued reading, frantically trying to piece together the ramblings scrawled there by a man seventy years ago. "The others that came here with him, the other prisoners, most were killed during the experiments, he...he could hear them dying, their screams, how one pleaded for mercy, begged for his mother but..."

Despite the fire, it seemed to get darker just then.

"He...he says something about evil, they—they're bringing Hell here, they're trying to...Jesus...most of this is really hard to read or make sense of, he...he's talking about them bringing these things here..."

"Things?"

Herm looked away from the wall and over at the others. "Demons."

"The entities you were talking about," Gino said. "These fuckers were doing rituals and experiments that conjured fucking *demons*?"

"There's no such thing," Quinn said.

"You sure about that?"

"Are you seriously telling me you—"

"I don't know. These guys were seeing something."

"They put this man in a cell and left him there," she reminded him. "Watched him slowly die with no food or water, watched him lose his mind and eventually his life, studying the process to see how long it took and how it played out. By the time he was writing these things he was probably already completely out of his mind."

"No," Herm said, turning back to the scrawls, moving the torch slowly in an attempt to read more. "No, he wasn't, he—I don't think he was, Quinn, he—he knew he was dying, he knew he was losing it but that's why he was scratching these things into the walls, he—he needed to tell what he was seeing and hearing and experiencing, even if he thought no one would ever see it. He needed to get it out, maybe—maybe it was the only way he could process it himself. They could look in on him through the slot in the door, but he could look out too. And he did. He saw things, he—he heard and witnessed things—he may have gone crazy but what he's saying, it...it fits with the things I've read before. He's talking about how they figured out how to bring these things here through the pain and torture but they couldn't...they couldn't..." He kept reading, bending down to follow a series of lines near the floor. "Those photographs, it makes sense, it—he's saying—I mean, it's in bits and pieces and it rambles into other things here and there, it—it doesn't always make perfect sense, okay? The poor bastard wrote this over what was probably weeks, and he only had a rudimentary grasp of Japanese he'd picked up over time, but the gist, far as I can tell, is they were able to make these entities—whatever the hell they were—manifest, and once they did, the subject, the—the ones who saw them—were invaded."

"That's why they looked possessed," Gino said. "Because they were."

186

Herm nodded vigorously. "Yeah, they—it didn't work, it—they couldn't control these things. Once inside the subjects they tore them apart—or they tore themselves apart, it—it's not clear, I mean, a lot of this makes no sense, it—"

"And this does?" Quinn asked.

"Look, there's a lot of this I can't even make out, but I'm pretty sure what he means here," Herm said, running a finger along one section of cell wall, "is they started to try the same thing but with dead bodies. It didn't work with the living, so they tried it with the recently dead to…"

"Animate them?" Dallas asked softly.

Quinn shot him a look. "Not you too. You're buying into this?"

"He's written 'It's Coming' at least ten times here. He says they kept trying to conjure something specific from the others they tried, something big…a…a warrior spirit…but it didn't work." Herm looked up at them, his face twisted with terror and disbelief. "Until it did."

"The man was out of his mind. And there's something else. It almost seems too perfect. Like maybe we were supposed to find all this."

"You're overthinking it, Quinn, getting paranoid. Trust me, nobody wanted this place found." Flame from the torch moved across Herm's face. "Remember when I told you that with the Japanese the wall between the spirit world and this one is much thinner than in our culture? In the beliefs of many—and even more so back then—there's a long history of bringing the dead back, of them returning as both protective and vengeful spirits, do you understand? That's what this man

187

was saying, that's what he's telling us all these years later. They figured out that when human beings are tortured and deprived of most if not all of their senses and they're being introduced to levels of pain and abuse beyond anything we're designed to handle, and likely being given mind-altering drugs on top of it, slowly, as the body breaks and the mind follows, the subjects begin to see these things. Just like the subjects did in the Nazi's experiments and those that were used in the MK-Ultra tests. Supposedly, once these entities manifested, not only the subjects saw them, but those conducting the tests did too. These things somehow passed from the spirit world to ours, or maybe it was an interdimensional thing, I—I don't know, I know it sounds insane, but I'm pretty sure they were trying to conjure demonic warrior spirits in this place, vengeful spirits that would protect and serve them. Ultimate soldiers, in a sense. No feelings, no remorse or morality, just a blind loyalty to protect and avenge. They tried it with living subjects, but it didn't work because they couldn't be contained, and these things tore their hosts to shreds. So they tried it with dead bodies. And it worked. At least once, it worked. That's what this poor sonofabitch witnessed as they slowly starved him to death. The result was a killing machine. Pure rage and violence. And that's exactly what this thing would have been."

"Would've been?" Gino asked. "Or still is?"

"We've already established none of these people could still be alive," Quinn said.

"If this is real," Herm said, "it's not alive. Not really."

188

"Whoever's out there isn't a spirit or some fucking ghost!" Quinn snapped. "It's physical, it's flesh and blood! It killed Murdoch!"

"It's using the physical…a body long dead, it—"

"Do you hear yourself?"

"Maybe possession alters physical limitations, slows down the decaying process or something, alters it somehow, I have no fucking idea."

"This is real life, Herm."

"Thank you, Quinn, for that amazing bit of in-depth analysis."

"Oh, fuck you. This is ridiculous. I know you're scared. I am too. But this is crazy horror movie bullshit. This is fantasy. This is fucking *insane*. You're taking literally the scribblings of a madman who was—"

"Wait." Herm came up out of his crouch and stumbled right by Quinn and out of the cell. "Harper, you—you saw this fucking thing."

Harper winced and grabbed hold of Gino.

"Focus up, goddamn it," Herm growled. "You need to answer me."

Gino pulled himself free of her. "Do what he says, honey."

Herm began to pace, trying to put his thoughts together, his mind reeling. "You said it looked like a monster, that it had horns and it looked like it was covered in metal. Right? That's what you said, isn't it?"

Harper said nothing, but nodded slowly.

"Could those horns have been part of a helmet? Could the metal you saw have been *armor*? Think back to what you saw."

She shrugged and began to tremble.

"Damn it, is that what you saw?"

"What are you on to?" Dallas asked.

"I got a…a theory maybe, a…an idea, I…I don't know but…" Herm turned away from her, pacing again nervously. "Okay…Okay… just hear me out a second, I—I think I may have something here. One of the more prominent protective and vengeful spirits in the Japanese culture are the spirits of great samurai warriors, okay? I'm thinking out loud here, so go with me. If you go back to traditional samurai warriors of the, say, the seventeenth century, when they're in full regalia, they're… they'd be…they're horrifying. Squares of metal body armor, iron helmets with horns—basically a kind of stylized deer antler kind of thing—ah, face—faceplates of iron or leather, sometimes both. That's exactly what they looked like. They were deadly, highly skilled killers, and the most prominent weapon they carried was a huge sword. The Empire would've had access to these historical things, and if this *worked*, like the shit all over these walls says it did…then…then maybe they couldn't control this thing so they just cut and ran. Or the war ended and they abandoned the place. I don't know, maybe they purified the ground where it was conjured but it didn't work. I'm saying…"

"What?" Gino pressed. "You're saying *what?*"

Herm's shoulders slumped and he hung his head. "I—I don't know what the hell I'm saying because it makes no sense and Quinn's right, it's—"

"Say it anyway."

Herm removed his glasses and wiped perspiration from his face with his free hand. "This thing, maybe it went to sleep. Or something like sleep. And when we came here, all these years later, it woke up. And now it's doing what it was designed to do, protecting this island with a level of vengeance and violence we can't even imagine. It slaughters anything that gets in its way or comes across its path."

"Not really alive," Gino said. "Not exactly dead."

Herm nodded, his face drawn and eerie in the remaining torchlight. "Caught somewhere between this world and wherever the hell it came from."

"This can't be real," Dallas muttered.

"I know," Herm said. "But I think it is."

"Then Harper was right." Gino wrapped an arm around her waist and pulled her against him. "It is a monster."

"We need to figure this out," Quinn said evenly, "but the torches are dying, we have to leave. Last thing we want is to be stuck here in the dark."

For a few seconds, no one moved or spoke. It was as if they all needed a moment for their bodies to catch up, to react while their minds crawled slowly back toward what they'd always believed was reality.

"Make sure you grab those rifles on the way out," Gino finally said. "Even if we can't get them into working order or find ammo, we can use the materials. Now let's move while we've still got fire."

In a daze of sorts, they moved back into the corridor, collecting the rifles as they made their way back through the series of rooms and toward the exit. As they got closer, light from the partially open main door spilled into the darkness.

But there was something else.

Thunder, rolling and booming across the heavens.

"There's a storm moving in," Gino said. "Hurry."

They stepped out into the light, their eyes adjusting as a strong wind blew in off the ocean. Lightning blinked, crackled somewhere nearby in the jungle.

"All right, we make a break for the commanding officer's quarters before the rain starts falling and we ride it out there. Won't be time to save the fire on the beach, so make sure you keep those torches alive until we get inside. We'll burn something or get a small fire going once we're in. Let's go."

They moved toward the building directly across from them.

And then the screaming began.

Dallas's mouth fell open in horror. He knew what he was seeing—what they were all seeing—but it didn't seem possible. It couldn't be.

Harper continued screeching and crying at the top of her lungs.

"No," Quinn gasped. "*No.*"

Three nude bodies had been strung up and secured to the flag pole and now dangled from it, filthy and savaged. One was in two pieces.

One was missing an arm. All had been mutilated, their skin raw, their eyes removed. Two bodies were male. Both had their severed members stuffed into their mouths.

"It dug them up," Herm shouted above the storm, his mind descending into chaos. "Jesus *Christ*, it dug them up!"

Thunder cracked, and rain began to fall, as above them, in a nightmare of blood, gore and body parts, the bodies of Natalie, Andre and Murdoch hanged suspended like the demonic trophies they'd become.

Harper screamed for her mother. Then her father. And finally, God.

None answered. There was only madness.

Madness and a violent, driving rain.

CHAPTER TWELVE

If they'd had the chance, if they'd been afforded the luxury of looking back on what had happened, how things had unfolded and gone from bad to worse, they'd have looked to that moment, that point where everything inside them broke, and all the things they thought they'd believed in, not only about the world and everyone in it, but themselves, had shattered. But they never got that chance. All they had was horror, the realization that live or die, they were being stalked by something relentless and beyond their comprehension. From that point forward, nothing was ever right again, because not only had their reality changed, *they* had changed as well. The people they'd been back in the world no longer existed. They were already dead.

"Go!" Dallas screamed, his voice booming above Harper's squeals. "Go! Run!"

They ran for the officers' quarters, Gino bolting into the lead, still holding Harper by the hand and dragging her along with him. Dallas and Quinn followed close behind, and Herm stumbled along at the back of the pack, fumbling with his dying torch and still unable to look away from the carnage hanging on display above them.

Wind and rain shook the jungle. Or was that the sound of something hulking through the brush instead, something barreling straight for them?

It was only when Gino let out a loud grunt, vaulted forward, and his grip was torn free from Harper, that the others snapped back into the moment. He'd collapsed violently and straight down into the earth, but in the confusion, panic and terror, it took several seconds for them to realize exactly what had happened.

The ground had swallowed Gino to the waist.

As he struggled to free himself, his hands clutching at anything he could find on either side of the hole he'd fallen into in a frenzied attempt to prevent himself from falling completely through, he shrieked in pain, releasing the kind of instinctually agonizing cry that signaled something was very wrong.

Quinn knew the sound well. As an EMT, she'd heard it before, and recognized it immediately for what it was, the involuntarily wail of someone seriously injured. No one screamed like that because they chose to, it was a reflexive response when confronted with a level of suffering they had no other answer for.

She stumbled to a stop, nearly pitching forward herself, then regained her balance, letting her torch drop to the ground as she reached for him.

GREG F. GIFUNE

Joining her, Herm grabbed hold of Gino's other hand, and together, they began pulling him free. He didn't come easily, but they were able to get him back up and out of the hole, his screams again cutting the sound of a now relentless rain.

"Harper!" Dallas called from somewhere behind them. "Goddamn it, Harper!"

Gino clamped onto Quinn with such power and strength it was painful, but the moment he was pulled free of the hole she understood why. His left leg, just below the knee, was bent forward and at an unnatural angle, and a small section of bloody shin bone protruded horrifically from his torn flesh.

"The fire!" he growled through gritted teeth and unbearable agony. "Save the fire, don't let it go out!"

"It's too late," Quinn told him, turning to Herm. "Help me get him up! We have to get him out of here!"

As they lifted him, Gino cried out again. "My leg, my—Jesus Christ—my leg!"

"Look at me," Quinn said. "Look at me! Hang on, we've got you!"

Gino tried, but his screams had already turned to sobs, and then his eyes rolled to white and he slipped from consciousness.

The rain was so strong it not only hurt on impact, it made visibility extremely difficult. The wind had increased as well, and by the time Dallas reached the jungle he was having trouble both seeing and hearing above the roar of the storm. He could hear the faintest screams in the distant, behind him and in the general area from which he'd come, but he kept moving. Harper was just up ahead of him, stumbling and staggering through the thick jungle, but he was closing the gap, swinging the machete to clear his way when he needed to without slowing his pace. He called to her to stop but she didn't acknowledge him.

It wasn't until she tripped and fell at the base of a large tree wrapped in thick vines that he was able to catch her, sliding down onto his knees before her. Harper had already curled into a fetal position, so he grabbed her arm and yanked her upright with his free hand.

"Get up!" he screamed above the storm. "We have to go back!"

She looked at him, but there was nothing in her eyes. Harper was gone.

"*Please*," he said, looking around quickly. "We have to get out of here! Please, get up! I didn't come all this way to leave you here! Come on!"

Her dead eyes shifted, moved beyond him. Then they widened in what Dallas first thought was confusion but quickly realized was terror.

There was something behind him.

With cold fear slithering along his spine, Dallas turned and looked back over his shoulder.

❖

The rain continued to fall, soaking them as Quinn and Herm propped Gino up and hurried as best they could across the outpost to the building that had once housed the officers' quarters. They dragged him inside, and the three collapsed to the floor together in a heap, out of breath.

"Fuck!" Herm gasped, wiping his mouth as he stared at the bone protruding from Gino's leg. "Is he…did he…"

"He's just unconscious."

"I—I've never seen a broken bone that bad."

Quinn forced herself up, stumbling back to the doorway. The rain fell in curtains, pummeling the island without mercy. She wiped hair from her eyes. "Where are they?"

"Harper took off into the jungle. Dallas went after her."

"Shit!" Quinn started out but Herm grabbed her arm.

"Quinn, you—"

She jerked free of him. "Get off me!"

Herm held his hands up and took a step back.

"We can't just leave them out there," she said.

"We can't go running after them without knowing what we're doing either. We don't know where they are, Quinn, we can't take the chance."

"I'll go."

"He never should've gone after her stupid ass."

"But he did."

"Yeah, he did. And we need to be smarter than that."

"We need to—"

"What we need to do is get those things we left behind. We have nothing to defend ourselves with. If whatever's out there comes for us, we're far too vulnerable. We *need* those weapons."

The rifles and ax lay scattered about where they'd dropped them in the confusion. And the hole Gino had fallen into, another apparent tunnel entrance, open wide now like the mouth of some giant predator, offered nothing but more horror.

"That's my husband out there. What I *need* to do is find him."

Gino groaned and writhed about a moment but never regained consciousness.

"Can you help him?" Herm asked.

"I can try, but..."

She didn't have to say anything more.

"Fuck it," Herm said. "You stay with Gino. I'll go."

"No, I'll—"

"*Quinn*." Herm took her by the shoulders, turned her toward him. "I'll go."

"We'll go together."

Before he could object further, she darted into the storm.

Despite everything he thought he knew, everything Herm had told them and the things in his mind he'd conjured as a result, nothing could have prepared him for the physical reality of what was bursting through the jungle and coming right for him.

A hideous smell preceded it, and instinctually, Dallas scrambled up off his knees and to his feet, shielding Harper with his body while raising the machete up above his head in as threatening a manner as he knew how.

But even then, this *thing* was too overwhelming to make sense of. It was there, right in front of him, and yet, his mind refused to believe what his eyes were seeing. Too much to process, it came in strange flashes—glimpses—bits and pieces coming at him through the rain like the nightmare it was.

It moved quickly, with deadly efficiency, the armor old and faded and looking like a second skin of battered metal squares. Horns extended monstrously from a helmet atop the enormous frame, beneath which a worn faceplate hid most of its decayed, scarred and leathery skin, its eyes burning red as blood, hands clutching a huge sword leveled in front of the being, as if pointing at him, an appendage reaching for its prey.

Like when he'd been in the water, his mind told him once again that this was only a game. He was coming up out of the surf, running along the sand and following the sweet sound of Quinn's voice. And then there she was. His love. His everything. So beautiful and strong and smart, running toward him with such joy. That's what he remembered most. The joy. Hers, and all that she brought him over the years. No one—*nothing*—could ever take that from him. He remembered them coming together on the beach, their bodies so desperately clinging to each other, so grateful they were both alive and all right and together again. He told her in his mind that he'd wait for her. One day, she'd find herself in an ocean as well, afraid and lost and tumbling through the waves. But she'd find land, and across the hot sand, she'd search for him until they found each other. And they'd be together again. This time for good.

This time forever.

It all happened rapidly, within a matter of seconds, but to Dallas it unfolded in slow-motion, and in that awful moment of terror and confusion, disbelief and finally, realization, he let Quinn go, felt her slip free of him.

Then there it was, standing right before him, glaring down at him through the rain with those horrible blood-red eyes.

202

GREG F. GIFUNE

Sliding around the gaping tunnel hole, fearful something might pop up out of it at any second, Herm gathered the rifles, slinging one over his shoulder and carrying the other. If nothing else, he could use it as a club, he thought.

Quinn slowed just long enough to scoop up the ax Gino had dropped then continued sprinting toward the jungle.

Herm did his best to catch up, but she was a considerable distance from him within seconds, already well into the jungle before he'd even gotten that far. Despite the pain in his pounding chest and the rain blurring his glasses, he stumbled on through the muddy earth and into the jungle after her.

Harper watched as Dallas raised the machete high, but the sword was already in motion. Fluid, and with inhuman speed, the blade rose, turned and swept down and across him, then back, up and down again in one continuous arcing motion, slashing Dallas on the initial swing and again on the follow-through.

Hot blood spattered her face, sprayed into her mouth and

burned her eyes.

The machete fell to the mud as Dallas dropped to his knees then fell forward onto his hands in another spray of blood.

Harper blinked away blood and rain.

Dallas attempted to rise, but couldn't. He said something, but she couldn't make it out over the storm.

The being widened its stance, raised the sword then brought it down again, this time with a single violent swing that separated Dallas's head from the rest of his body.

The head rolled away, trailing gore, his eyes still open and staring into eternity with disbelief and horror, as the body collapsed into the bloody mud.

Harper closed her eyes and waited for the blade to take her as well.

By the time Herm reached the small clearing and saw Harper sitting beneath the tree, Quinn was already on the ground, kneeling next to Dallas's body, head bowed and her entire body bucking with each wailing sob.

Christ, he thought, *there's no head, his—his head's missing.*

"Baby," Quinn sobbed. "My baby, my...my baby..."

"No." Herm moved closer, emotion getting the better of him as well. Tears of horror and rage and pain filled his eyes, and he whirled around, looking for whatever had done this. Harper knew. That mindless, useless, stupid little bitch knew. Just like before, she knew. "No! Mother*fucker*, no!"

Harper just sat there, staring straight ahead like a mannequin covered in blood.

Quinn rose, the ax in her bloody hands and her wet hair plastered against her face. Something had changed in those once beautiful eyes. Something raging and cold, evil and heartless resided there now. Something ready to do battle. To kill without mercy or remorse. She glanced back at Herm, who stood there stupidly, unsure of what to say or do, then took a few steps further into the jungle.

Perhaps forty yards or so in the distance, on a small ridge of ground, the being stood watching them through the heavy rain. It held a sword in one hand, and a human head in the other.

A primal, horrible scream tore through the jungle.

It wasn't until the thing slipped away into the cover of thick brush that Herm realized the scream had come from Quinn, who had bent forward at the waist and screeched at the being with a rage he'd never known human beings possessed, her eyes wide and wild, spittle dripping and hanging from her lips in long drools, her husband's blood all over her.

The rain kept coming.

Herm reached down, none-too-gently grabbed Harper by the wrist and yanked her to her feet. She offered no resistance. There wasn't enough left of her to do anything but stand there like the near-empty shell she'd become. "Quinn," he said. When she didn't respond or face him, he said it again, but louder. "Quinn!"

This time she turned, the same look in her bloodshot eyes.

"We have to go."

"I'm going after it."

"Not like this. You'll die."

The look on her face made it abundantly clear she didn't care.

"We need you," Herm told her. "Gino needs you."

Quinn turned back to the jungle, said nothing.

"We have to—"

"Go back, Herm," she said evenly. "Take that moron that cost my husband his life and go back to Gino."

"I'm not leaving you alone out here."

She sank down to her knees, suddenly, as if she could no longer prevent her body from doing so, and with head bowed, wept over Dallas's body.

In that oddly surreal moment, a break that had begun much earlier in him became complete as well. Nothing mattered now. It was all about the most primordial instincts now, nothing more. In some ways they were no different than that thing out there. And maybe that was best, because it was necessary to survive, and survival, for however long they could cling to it, was the only thing they had left.

They were savages now, nothing more.

Pawing rainwater from his eyes, he looked Harper up and down. Her skimpy, filthy, soaked and worn white bikini left virtually nothing to the imagination now. With his free hand he roughly grabbed one of her breasts, squeezing and shaking it violently, pinching then pulling the nipple. She stared into the distance, offering neither objection nor resistance. She was either no longer capable of realizing what was happening to her, or simply didn't care. Regardless, it stirred something deep inside him, something that made him want to dominate and hurt her, to fuck her like the animals they were.

He looked over at Quinn to make sure she hadn't seen what he'd done.

She hadn't, and was now slumped over the body, her cries muffled.

We're all going to die, Herm thought. *All of us.*

CHAPTER THIRTEEN

Herm stood in the open doorway, watching the jungle through the rain and his own uncontrollable tears. Behind him, Harper sat in the corner just where he'd left her, silent and staring into oblivion. Gino had regained consciousness twice but only for short intervals, slipping away quickly each time. A rifle still slung over his shoulder, in his hands, Herm held the machete, its blade and handle still covered in Dallas's blood and tissue. For several minutes he'd tried to work every scenario he could imagine, fighting his way through the tsunami of emotions coursing through him. What if Quinn didn't come back? What then? He remembered the look in her eyes, the rage, and couldn't help but wonder, what if she did? He couldn't shake the vision of Dallas's headless body lying there in the mud.

"My..." His voice caught in his throat. "You were my friend," he said softly, quickly wiping his tears. His face drifted through Herm's mind, his smile, memories of the times they'd spent together. Not many people had ever been kind to him, but Dallas had always treated him with respect and as a true friend. Herm had never felt like he deserved it, and even less so now, because Dallas had died the way he lived, as the best of them. "It's okay, man," he whispered. "It's okay now. You're free."

But it wasn't okay. Not for the rest of them. The past, good and safe times they'd known, it was all over now. Everything was over now.

Breaking through the jungle, Quinn emerged, moving in long, purposeful strides through the pouring rain, her face stone. Clutching the ax, she moved across the outpost without looking his way, and closed on the two smaller structures they'd earlier surmised were most likely used as storage units. Both huts had been largely reclaimed by the jungle, wrapped heavily in vines and plant growth, but without hesitation and barely slowing her stride, Quinn swung the ax at them again and again, and with each angry and violent swing, more and more overgrowth was cleared.

Herm let the rifle slide off his shoulder, placed it on the floor then staggered down the remains of the porch and into the rain. Even when he joined her, Quinn never stopped or acknowledged him. Using the machete, he began to help. There was something incredibly freeing and cathartic about swinging that giant blade, slamming it down into the vines and growth without remorse, hesitation or even the slightest concern, and with each blow, he felt something inside him stirring, growing, empowering him with things he never knew he had inside him.

When most of the brush and vines had been hacked apart, Quinn stuck the ax into the mud then began ripping it free and tossing it aside. Herm continued helping, using the machete to cut away the last of the clinging vines until the two small huts were accessible.

They both waited a moment, breathing heavily as the rain soaked them down. At one point they made eye contact, and that was enough. No other words needed to be spoken just then.

Taking up the ax again, Quinn smashed the doors to each hut.

As they'd suspected, they were used for storage. One housed nothing but a series of large sealed drums. Gasoline. The second was filled with various supplies, and boxes of ammunition piled on the floor, and a series of makeshift shelves fully stocked with old rations, cans of various food and tins of rice meant to last for long periods of time in the field. On the floor was a large crate, the top pried off long ago. It had once been filled with grenades, but now there were only four.

Though she'd never handled such things, Quinn grabbed the grenades without hesitation and started back to the officers' quarters. Herm tucked the machete in his pants, gathered as much food as he could carry then hurried along behind her, checking the jungle as he went to make sure that thing hadn't reappeared.

At the entrance, along the railing around the remains of the porch, several of the small containers they'd found and positioned about as rain-catchers were overflowing. Quinn took one, drank it down then returned it to the railing. The second she brought with her into the quarters.

Once inside, Herm placed all the cans and tins on the floor then hurried outside. He returned with a container full of rainwater. After squatting down and offering it to Harper, who refused, he took a long drink himself.

"Be careful with those grenades, they're more than likely still live," he said, his voice barely audible above the rain. "Some of this food's probably edible. Won't have much taste, I wouldn't think, but—"

"Hold him."

Herm forced a swallow. "What?"

Quinn knelt down next to Gino, who was barely conscious, and placed the ax alongside her, still within reach. "Hold him," she said again, pouring water from one of the rain-catchers over her hands, cleaning them as best she could.

"Quinn, I—"

"*Hold* him."

When Herm looked into Gino's eyes, for the first time he saw nothing but pain and fear. Taking him by the shoulders, he pressed down with all his weight then gave Quinn a nod.

"A compound fracture has a higher risk of complications and infection," she said flatly, as if reading from a manual. "I need to wash it out, get the dirt and loose bone fragments out, make the wound clean as possible. Then I have to position the bones, put them back into place, realign them, and apply a splint to keep them stable."

Gino, who had broken out in a heavy sweat, nodded groggily, his eyes barely open. "Do what you have to do," he said, his voice weak and slurred.

212

The screams began the moment she poured water into the open wound and began scooping out the unattached fragments of bone. She worked meticulously and without emotion, ignoring his cries and begs for her to stop as she followed her training and, gently as she could, took the snapped bone between her fingers and pushed it back down into place.

As she realigned the bones, Gino's screams finally ceased and he passed out. Once his body had gone limp Herm let him go and sat back, hands to his head. He'd never heard anyone, male or female, scream like that.

Blood bubbled up out of the wound, draining residual dirt and bone chips.

Quinn removed his tank top, wrung it out then wrapped the wound with it. Standing, she wiped her eyes and face and drew a few deep breaths. Then she grabbed an overturned chair and smashed it to pieces. Taking two flat chunks of wood that had once constituted part of the seat, she positioned them on either side of Gino's shin and instructed Herm to hold them in place.

Once he'd taken over, she left, returning a moment later with two long lengths of heavy vine, which she used to wrap and tie the pieces of wood to Gino's leg.

"He's fucked," Herm said. "Isn't he."

"We're all fucked."

"Quinn, I—"

"Don't." She wiped the blood and fluids staining her hands on her shorts, adjusted the cups of her bikini top, then took the old tin of water Herm hadn't finished, and held it out to Harper.

"Labels are all faded, and they're in Japanese anyway," he said a moment later, "but we've got food here, such as it is. Rice, most likely, probably some kind of meat. Beans, maybe some fruit. Won't know until we crack it open."

Quinn pushed the water at Harper again, but she looked right past her.

"She's done," Herm said. "There's nobody home."

Crouching, Quinn put the container to Harper's lips and poured some into her mouth. Most dribbled out over her bottom lip. "Make sure Gino gets water." She handed the cup to Herm. "Even if he's unconscious, wet his lips with it." She grabbed her ax. "When he wakes up, give him small sips. He probably won't stay awake long, but when he does wake up, make sure he drinks."

"Where are you going?"

"To take watch." She looked out the doorway to the jungle. "We're going to do what Gino said. Defend our position."

"What if it doesn't come?"

"It will."

"What if it doesn't?"

"Then we'll go find it…flush it out into the open…and kill the fuck."

214

"I'm not sure it's alive."

"To do what's it doing, what it's done, it has to be alive in some sense." She watched the rain a while. "And if it's alive, that means it can die."

"How do you kill something that's already dead?"

"You annihilate it," she said in monotone, "eradicate it from existence."

"And how do we do that?"

Quinn gave no answer, just kept watching the rain and jungle.

"What happens when it gets dark?" he pressed. "No more fire, no light."

"We wait. We watch the night. We defend our position." Hoisting the ax up and over her shoulder, she finally looked down at him. "Or we die trying."

"We're gonna die anyway," he said softly.

"Yeah." Quinn moved to the doorway, her back to him. "I know."

It's the beauty she remembers most. The sun, the way his hand felt in hers.

They stand at the water's edge, watching the waves slowly roll in, gently lap the sandy beach at their bare feet. Overhead, seagulls caw and circle, some landing on a nearby stone jetty, others riding the waves further out. The sea air is crisp and clear, the breeze off the ocean refreshing. The heat is high but there is little humidity. The perfect day, she thinks. The perfect day with the perfect man.

As if he can read her mind, he looks at her and makes a funny face, the kind he's made for years that always makes her laugh even though she's seen it thousands of times.

Okay, she thinks, maybe not perfect, but close enough.

She remembers it all, this day, their conversations, their leisurely walk along the beach, watching the birds and the waves, and for long stretches just holding hands and saying nothing at all. It is in those quiet moments where she realizes how deep her love for her husband is. There is no need for words or gestures, the simple act of being together is enough. Together, they are whole.

What she doesn't remember, is the white clothing both wear. Even as the visions unfold before her, she questions it. She remembers wearing jean shorts, a tank top and sandals. She remembers him wearing khakis, sneakers and a t-shirt. So why are they both clad in white, knee-length hospital johnnies?

They would never wear such things, but neither seem to care.

After a long winter, the sun is back, the warmth has returned, and since the beach is within walking distance of their home, it is a trip they like to make often, before summer is in full swing and the beach becomes crowded and noisy, a different experience altogether.

216

GREG F. GIFUNE

As a little girl, she read all the fairytales, heard all the love stories.

Now, she's as close to living one as she will likely ever get. Their life together may not be perfect, but they're happy—genuinely happy—and that's more than most can say.

"You're such a romantic," he tells her, smiling gently.

"And you're not?"

He shrugs. "There are worse things."

"Guilty of some of those too."

They laugh, snuggle closer and continue walking along the beach, feet sinking in the wet sand.

"I love you," she tells him.

They stop, he takes her face in his hands and kisses her the way he always does. First her forehead, then the tip of her nose and finally, her lips. "Love you too."

And then it all goes wrong. Something is wrong, something… something is wrong and she doesn't know what it is but she can feel it moving through her like a snake, coiling and nesting within her.

Something falls from the sky.

The birds. They're falling from the sky. One, and then another.

On fire, they plummet to the earth all around them in balls of flame.

"The birds, they—they're on fire, they…"

Blood seeps through their white gowns, soaking them down and plastering against them like a second skin.

She reaches for him, her fingers dripping blood…

The look of love on his face turns to terror and confusion as he lets her go and slowly backs away, the birds crashing all around him in a rain of fire.

She reaches for him again, but he is already too far away.

Someone screams. She can't be sure who.

It's you, Quinn.

She closes her eyes, hoping it's all a bad dream and that when she opens them everything will be back to normal.

But there is only darkness. Endless, bottomless darkness...

Wake up, Quinn. Wake up.

The jungle slowly came into focus.

It took a moment, but Quinn soon realized she'd fallen asleep and had just then come awake. As it hit her, she found herself sitting in the doorway, facing the jungle, the ax lying across her lap. Back on her feet, she shook her head, hoping to dislodge the cobwebs, and looked around frantically. The heavy rain had stopped, but it was misting out, draping the island in a strange early morning fog she'd not seen here prior.

Gino lay where she'd left him, but he was awake and looking at her.

She couldn't believe she'd not only allowed herself to fall asleep,

218

but she'd evidently slept for hours. A stupid mistake that could've cost her and the others their lives, she thought. Wiping her mouth, she moved over to Gino and knelt next to him.

"I thought I died," he said groggily. "During the night. I thought I died."

Quinn's hand found his forehead, confirming what she already knew from the look of him. He was burning up, drenched in sweat, and his skin had gone white as chalk. Still unable to believe she'd fallen asleep, Quinn rubbed her eyes, then gave Gino a few sips of water.

"Shouldn't waste it on me."

"Just drink it."

"I have a fever, don't I?"

Quinn inspected his leg wound. It was seeping blood and oozing other fluids. "You'll be all right," she lied. "Just rest."

"Can you get me up?"

"Gino, you're too weak and your leg's badly broken. You can't stand."

His frustration and sorrow palpable, he nodded. "Help me sit up at least?"

"You should just—"

"I don't want to die flat on my back, Q. Not like that."

"You're not going to die."

"Help me."

"It's going to hurt."

"Already hurts."

Taking him under the arms, Quinn lifted him enough to slide him over to an old file cabinet a foot or so away. He cried out, groaned then went quiet as she leaned him against it, carefully propping him up.

Sitting back on her heels, she took in the rest of the room in the low morning light, and realized they were the only two there. "Where's Herm? Where's Harper?"

Gino's head slumped forward. He'd passed out again.

Ax in hand, Quinn returned to the doorway and looked out at the outpost and surrounding jungle. Nothing. No one.

Moving down across the porch, heart racing and the sleep that had clung to her in these last few moments finally burning away, she forced memories of the nightmare from her mind and focused on the task at hand. Creeping around the side of the building, she watched and waited, bracing herself for whatever might come at her. But there was nothing there. She was alone.

Sprinting toward the lagoon, she made it to the sand and took in as much area as she could. But still, nothing, and no sign of either Herm or Harper.

"Where the hell are they?" she muttered.

Suspicious silence answered.

The mist moved along with the fog, making visibility difficult and giving the island a surreal, dreamlike look and feel. As if still caught in her nightmare, Quinn crept through the fog, searching for any trace of the others.

A strange noise froze her in mid-step. She listened. There it was again. An odd muffled sound somewhere between a moan and a growl. Definitely human and most likely male, but she couldn't be sure of much else.

Stepping through a bank of fog and into a row of palm trees at the edge of the sand, she hesitated, and heard it again. She was only about thirty yards or so from the lagoon itself, and as they did each morning and every early evening, the sharks had returned, their fins breaking the surface of the water now and then as they cruised about in slow circles.

The sound grew louder, more aggressive, then faded.

This time it sounded vaguely familiar, but…it couldn't be…

The mist drifted by her, separating enough for her to see the machete stuck into the trunk of a nearby palm tree, stabbed and left there purposely.

And at the base of the tree, two bodies.

Herm. On top of Harper. Her bikini had been discarded and tossed aside, and lie tangled in the sand a few feet away. Through the fog, Herm's pale and pockmarked ass rose then fell, again and again as he slammed himself between Harper's open legs, fucking her harder and harder with each thrust, his moans louder now, urgent.

Wrestling equal parts disbelief and nausea, Quinn moved closer, gripping the ax with such fury her hands ached.

"Stop," she heard herself say. "*Herm*. Stop!"

Gasping, he slammed into Harper again, coughed, then lie still atop her.

"Get off her. Now."

Herm rolled off. Still gasping for air, he got to his feet, pulling his tattered jeans up as he went. Staggering about a moment, he regained his balance and wiped spittle from the corner of his mouth. Lying nude in the sand, Harper remained where she was, legs spread wide and slick with cum, her eyes open and staring up at the sky, seeing nothing, feeling nothing.

"You fucking sonofabitch."

"Fuck off, Quinn." He glanced down at Harper. "She doesn't give a shit."

"Don't you?"

"No." He took a step toward her. "I don't."

"Get away from her."

"I wanted to fuck the stupid little bitch, so I did. Why not? Doesn't matter anyway. She doesn't even know where she is. Besides, we could all be dead any minute. Probably will be."

"Just…get away."

"I'm not done yet."

"Yeah. You are."

Herm chuckled and shook his head. "You know, at first I kept thinking they'd find us. Sooner or later they'd have to, right? Today's day

222

and age and all that. But you know what, Quinn? The more I thought about it and the worse things got, the more I realized the odds of us ever leaving this island were more or less nonexistent. And the more I thought about *that*, the more I realized maybe that didn't have to be such a bad thing. It's all in what we do, how we deal with it, see what I mean? Hell, what am I missing anyway? What do I want to go back to so badly? My empty apartment? My nowhere job and all those snot-nosed little fuckers who laugh at me behind my back—sometimes even right to my face—a world where I'm nobody, a fucking joke, and no one cares if I live or die? A world where women don't give me the time of day? A world where I'm essentially powerless? *That's* what I was jonesing to get back to?"

"Just get away from her, all right?"

"Nah. I don't think I will."

"You make me sick."

"Be that as it may, the way I see it, one of two things is gonna happen here. One, that thing out there is going to take us out one by one, just like it has the others, in which case we're all gonna die anyway, so who gives a shit? Or two, we figure out a way to stop it, to kill it before it kills us. And then, this island is ours. Or I guess I should say *mine*. Gino's fucked, we both know it. I stayed awake last night while you had your little nappy-poo, and watched him. Yeah. His big tough guy know-it-all days are over. He's burning up with fever, which means he's got an infection, which means it'll likely kill him. And this one," he scoffed, motioned to Harper. "She's a fucking vegetable. A vegetable with great tits, a hot little ass and a sweet pussy, no question, but still a fucking vegetable. She won't even take food or water anymore unless you force it on her. Dumb twat's gonna be dead in a matter of days, so why not get some? Back in the world, she would've laughed at me, looked at me like I wasn't even human. So fuck her. Literally. That pretty much just leaves you and me, Quinn. And this island. And that's all it leaves. For the rest of our fucking lives."

"You're out of your mind."

"Yeah, probably. We all are. Who could blame us after everything we've been through, right? Not really sure what that's got to do with anything. Point is, for however long I've got, minutes, hours, days, weeks, months or years, I'm not going to be the joke anymore, the weak one, the one nobody takes seriously. This island is mine. And for however long she lasts, so is this cretin. In time, you will be too, because there won't be anything *but* us." Herm smiled, straightened his wig. "So go back and play nursemaid to Gino while I finish up playing with this slut, and then we'll figure out what to do next."

Quinn shook her head no.

"Since when do you care, anyway? This ass cost Dallas his life and you're—"

"Don't you say his name," she snapped. "You don't deserve to say his name."

"You're right. He was the best of us, wasn't he? And look what it

224

got him. It's a new world, Quinn. Yours and mine. We either take it, or die trying. That's it. That's all there is now."

"Just get out of here. Go back and..."

"No can do." Scratching his beard, Herm looked down at Harper. "Few more things I want to do with my special lady friend here."

"I'm not fucking around, Herm." Quinn leveled the ax, raising enough to remind him she was carrying it. "Leave. Now."

"It doesn't matter anymore. *We* don't matter anymore. Get it?"

"You're not touching her again."

He stared at her for what seemed forever, the mist all around them and the fog moving between them like ghosts. "I've always liked and respected you, Quinn. Hell, truth be told, I've jacked off thinking about you over the years more times than I can remember. Used to feel guilty about it. Kind of. Now, not so much. So no more telling me what to do. The way things work now is, you don't tell me shit. I do what I want."

Herm reached for the machete, yanked it free of the palm tree. "Fuck off, Quinn, before this gets past a point we can't come back from."

"We're already there."

"What do you think you're gonna do?" He stepped closer, the machete down by his leg. "What do you think you *can* do to me? Huh?"

"Go back and keep watch. I'll take care of Harper and we'll—"

"I'm not going anywhere until I do everything I want to do to this cunt."

"I'll kill you if I have to."

Herm smiled. "What makes you think I won't kill you if *I* have to?"

"Get out of here."

"Why don't you come make me?" The machete held higher, he slowly began to circle her. "Come on, butch, let's see what you've got."

"We need each other, Herm."

"All the more reason for you to fuck off." He circled closer. "No more rules."

"I'm not going to let you do this to her."

"Then this must be the part where you try to stop me."

"You really have lost your mind."

With sudden and horrifying viciousness, Herm swung the machete.

Quinn leaned back and out of the way just in time, the blade missing her by inches. Stumbling away, she caught her balance and squared her stance, ax at the ready. "Okay," she said, gritting her teeth. "Okay. Come on."

They circled each other in the mist, the fog surrounding them.

As he lunged for her again, she blocked the blade with the ax, raising it up before her so the handle took the brunt of the machete strike. But he landed with such force it knocked her back and off her feet and tore the ax from her grip. Quinn fell onto the seat of her pants, stunned, the ax spiraling through the air and landing a few feet away.

She lunged for it, but before she could reach it Herm pounced, swinging the machete at her in wide, wild arcs.

She rolled away, scrambling back to her feet just in time to dodge another swing of the blade. As it whizzed by her face, she pivoted and kicked Herm in the knee with her heel.

Wailing, he staggered back but remained upright. Then he rushed her again.

This time Quinn was ready.

A two-punch combination landed before he could reach her, snapping his head back, breaking his glasses and dropping Herm to one knee. Blood trickled from his nose and split lip. He stood up, wiped at the blood then looked at his hand and smiled.

"Stop," Quinn said. "*Stop.*"

Tossing his glasses aside, he rushed her again, stabbing with the machete rather than swinging it this time, which backed her up along the sand and into another tree. She fell back against it, bracing herself and raising her hands in a gesture she hoped would make him stop.

But instead he swung the machete at her head.

She ducked and it struck the tree behind her, lodging in the trunk.

Hitting him first in the gut and then with an uppercut, she knocked him back, but Herm was tougher than he looked. With his wig askew, he grabbed hold of her by the throat and backed her against the tree, squeezing with such force she could no longer breathe and spittle began to bubble up and out of her mouth.

Slamming her fists down into the bends in his arms, she broke his grip, and gagging, dropped to her knees, struggling for breath, but Herm was on her again, this time grabbing her by the hair and slamming her head against the tree. As pain exploded through the back of her skull and a sunburst of colors exploded across her field of vision, she nearly lost consciousness.

He pulled her head forward, ready to slam it into the tree again, but Quinn stabbed a thumb deep into his eye.

Herm yelped, staggered back and doubled over, his hands covering his face.

Quinn stood near the tree, swaying and dizzy.

He came for her again, suddenly, and they both smashed into the tree, jockeying for position. As Quinn pushed her forearm under his chin and pushed hard as she could, she realized Herm was reaching behind her for the machete. With her other hand she grabbed his wrist, but he was too strong, and quickly yanked the blade from the trunk.

Still controlling his wrist, she used all her strength to prevent him from bringing it down onto her skull, but she knew she couldn't hold him off long. She brought a knee up into his crotch. He gasped, released her and dropped to his knees in pain.

Taking him by the shoulders, Quinn pulled him to his feet, spun him around and slammed him into the tree, driving him into it with a shoulder block to his midsection.

GREG F. GIFUNE

As he crashed into the tree, his head snapping back and slapping the trunk as well, Quinn reached down, grabbed the machete and cocked it back, holding it there a moment.

Herm's eyes widened, and he pushed off from the tree, lunging for her.

Before she fully realized what she'd done, Quinn had driven the machete straight into him. It penetrated his stomach with a sickening wet sound, and he gagged, grunting like the wounded animal he was.

The fog engulfed them, as if to hide their sins.

Quinn fell against him, and they stood there a moment in each other's arms, the blade buried deep in his gut, his blood flowing over them both. He looked into her eyes and tried to speak, but vomited blood instead, spraying her face and neck with it.

Wheezing, Herm fought to remain conscious, glaring into Quinn's eyes with disbelief and drooling dark blood out over his bottom lip.

Then he nodded, as if submitting and somehow granting her permission.

Quinn gripped the machete with both hands, and with a primal scream, ripped it up and over, tearing through what remained of his abdomen.

Another explosion of blood erupted from Herm's mouth and eyes, and he dropped to the sand, the machete still buried deep inside him.

He made gurgling sounds for a few seconds, convulsed then lay still, a large pool of black blood forming all around him and soaking into the sand.

Quinn stumbled back then dropped to her knees. Exhausted, her head spinning, sickness throttled her. As she vomited, behind her, Harper rose to her feet.

Quinn watched, still trying to catch her breath and grasp what had just happened.

Harper, or whoever—whatever—she was now, looked right through her, then turned and walked off across the sand and down to the lagoon, wide swaths of blood staining her thighs and buttocks.

By the time Quinn realized what she was doing it was too late, but she forced herself to her feet and stumbled after her anyway. "Harper!" she screamed.

She was already in waist deep water.

"Harper! No!"

She turned and faced Quinn. With a sad smile of temporary recognition, or perhaps just release, Harper fell straight back into the water.

Within seconds, the sharks had closed on her, and all Quinn could do was drop to the sand and watch as Harper was poked and prodded, and finally, bitten.

The approaches and attacks escalated quickly, and soon Harper's body was thrashing and jerking about like a ragdoll.

GREG F. GIFUNE

The lagoon turned a deep crimson, bubbling with carnage as her body vanished beneath the surface in a feeding frenzy of unimaginable gore and violence.

In time, everything went quiet again.

Mist and fog drifted out over the lagoon.

Quinn sat there a moment, numb. She wanted to cry, to rage, but realized she neither had the strength nor the capacity.

And then she realized something else.

She was not alone on the beach.

CHAPTER FOURTEEN

Even as she turned and rolled away, the enormous sword was falling toward her, striking the ground where she'd been and missing her by seconds. The attacker came to her in a blur of motion and panic, a large being with reptilian-like armor, a horned helmet and frightening faceplate, above which sat a pair of blood-red, rage filled eyes. It smelled like rotten garbage, and with each movement, the terrible stench grew worse.

Scrambling away in a crablike walk, Quinn scurried back, trying to regain her feet as the massive figure followed, swinging the sword with precision and violence.

In a frantic attempt to escape it, Quinn threw a handful of sand at the creature, hitting it full in the face and across the eyes. It stopped the thing a moment, and it shook its head, reaching for its eyes.

Quinn flipped over onto her hands and knees, crawled away quickly and eventually rose up and broke into a run, back toward the palm trees and Herm's body. Her ax lay in the sand not far from him, but by the time she'd gotten hold of it and looked back at the lagoon, the creature had already closed the distance and was only a few feet away, angling the samurai sword at her in a rapid sweeping motion.

She screamed, not in fear but rage, a wail of challenge and defiance.

The creature attacked.

She managed to block several blows with the ax handle, the steel blade clanging against the metal ax and sending her off her feet and onto the ground. She landed with such force it knocked most of the wind from her, and she realized then that she stood no chance against this thing. It was far too big, powerful, determined and skilled for her to fight.

As she got back to her feet, swinging the ax before her in a defensive mode she hoped would keep the creature at bay, it walked right into the path of the ax without concern. The ax struck its side, bouncing rather harmlessly off its armor and reverberating up Quinn's arms with such force that the ax was torn from her grip and flew several feet into the air in the other direction.

And then it had hold of her, it's gloved hand, covered in the same mesh-like armor across it's torso, clamping onto her neck and effortlessly pulling her up and off her feet.

Kicking and punching hard as she could, Quinn could still not break its grip, as it lifted her high into the air with one hand and shook her.

The next thing she knew, she was vaulting backwards in midair, flying across the sand and slamming into one of the nearby palm trees.

Collapsing into the sand, she rolled and came up on her knees. The ax was several feet away, the machete was trapped beneath Herm's body, and the creature was closing on her again.

There was no time, and she had no chance. If she tried to fight, this thing would surely kill her. Turning, Quinn rose and ran for the jungle.

Breaking through the nearest opening in the brush and running with all the strength she had left, she sprinted through the jungle. But she could hear it behind her, running too, getting closer and closer still. The smell grew stronger, and she could hear its armor and weaponry rattling. Fearing it was even closer than she realized, Quinn darted quickly to the right, felt her foot snag on something and suddenly she was airborne again, this time hurdling through the heavy jungle, the vines and leaves tearing at her as she landed and plummeted down a steep decline.

The world blurred and tumbled as she rolled along the slanted ground, the force of her body ripping through the brush with such speed she was unable to stop or even slow her momentum.

Eventually she hit a tree, slamming it with her shoulder. Stabbing pain exploded up into her neck and down along her spine as her body finally slowed and rolled to a stop at the bottom of the large slope. Aching and sore, her flesh torn and scratched from the brush,

Quinn struggled up into a kneeling position and looked back in the direction from which she'd come. The slope was steep and covered an area of seventy yards or more, which she'd descended in a matter of seconds.

She stayed still as possible and tried to listen. But the sound of her labored breath made it difficult to hear much of anything else. So she relied on her eyes. The jungle above was thick but the fog and mist had mostly dissipated here, and she was able to make out the top of the ridge from which she'd fallen.

Something separated from the surrounding jungle.

There it was. Standing at the summit in all its horror. A killing machine from another time, another place.

A chill coursed through her as its head turned one way and then the next. Slowly, it panned back and forth, moving past her position several times.

It doesn't see me, she thought.

Quinn remained perfectly still. Her body had become smeared with dirt and debris during the slide, and combined with the brush and vines hanging all around her, she was effectively concealed, at least for the moment. Though it was difficult, she tried to slow her breathing and even refrained from blinking as long as she could, her eyes set and staring directly up at the thing standing in the distance above her.

Just when she thought she'd found some hope, the thing turned and began descending the slope sideways, purposely but skillfully heading for her with a fluid, graceful gait.

There was no way she could outrun it, and she had even less chance fighting it, so Quinn lay back in the brush, burying herself in it as deeply as possible and hoping it might camouflage her. Lying alongside a rotted stump, she found softer ground, burrowed as far into it as she could then lay very still.

The creature descended the slope quickly, stopping less than ten feet from where she was hiding. The terrible stench wafted all around it, the smell of death and decay. It took a few steps to the left, then came back, moving more to the right.

Quinn lay covered in dirt and brush only a few feet away. She held her breath, despite the pain in her chest and shoulder, and forced her eyes closed. If it found her, she didn't want to see it coming.

Do it, you fuck. Just do it, get it over with. Kill me. Do it.

Brush by her head crackled and shifted beneath the creature's weight.

Instinctually, her eyes opened to see the lower legs and booted feet of the thing moving right by her. It strode deeper into the jungle, waited a moment then broke into a run, dashing off and out of sight.

Quinn let out her breath, her chest heaving and her entire body sore and aching as she rolled out from the side of the stump and crawled onto her hands and knees. She raised her head, watched the section of jungle the creature disappeared into.

It was gone. She was alive, and it was gone.

First she laughed, quietly, but soon came tears, muffled sobs she couldn't control. Exhausted and completely drained physically and emotionally, Quinn collapsed down into the dirt and brush, and lay there a while.

After a while, she forced herself back to her feet. It was then that she noticed a hole in the ground not far from where the thing had vanished. It had run into the jungle and again gone into the tunnels beneath the island.

Quinn wiped herself off then started back up the slope.

She knew now what she had to do.

After finding the ax, Quinn went to one of the larger basins they'd found at the outpost and left out to catch rain, dropped to her knees and drank as much as she could stand. The sun was rising, having burned off all the fog and mist, and the water had already turned lukewarm. She vomited the first several gulps, then went back for more.

Once sated, she looked out at the lagoon. All the blood had washed away.

It was as if Harper had never died there at all, as if she never even existed.

As Quinn made her way back toward the outpost, she noticed Herm's body had been disturbed. The machete was no longer in his abdomen but laying on the sand next to him. His wig had been left nearby as well. And where his head should've been, instead were scraps of flesh and a bloody stump of neck bone and protruding spine.

Feeling nothing now, Quinn bent down, picked up the bloody machete and continued on to the outpost.

Watching the jungle as best she could, and trying to make as little noise as possible, despite her exhaustion, she took hold of one of the large barrels of gasoline from the storage hut and dragged it to the mouth of the tunnel Gino had fallen into.

Using the machete, she wrenched the lid free and tossed it aside. The drums had been sealed all this time, and shielded from the elements inside the hut, so the gasoline likely hadn't been compromised and would still burn.

Leaning her weight against it and pushing with all her might, she tipped the drum over and watched as the gasoline emptied, rushing down into the tunnel. When it was nearly empty, she grabbed the end and tilted it far as she could until the remaining gas poured free.

Rolling it away, she returned to the hut, and dragged a second drum over to the hole. Once it had emptied into the tunnel, she headed into the officer's quarters.

Walking through the open doorway, she found Gino just where she'd left him, sitting up and propped against the old file cabinet. His broken leg was drenched in blood, the splint had come undone, and he was sweating profusely, one of the old Japanese rifles they'd found clutched in his hands as if it might somehow protect him.

The WWII food supplies Herm had found were scattered across the floor, as at one point Gino had apparently torn into a couple of tins. One lay on its side, what appeared to be beans of some kind emptied out onto the floor. There were also some hard candies and an open container of tea. Though Quinn hadn't eaten since the crab the night before last, for the first time since this ordeal began, her hunger was not an issue. Eating was the last thing she wanted to do, but knew going without was sapping what little energy she had left. She scooped up two of the hard candies. They were wrapped in a foil that had partially become stuck to them, but she managed to get them unwrapped and popped them in her mouth. She couldn't identify the flavor, if there was one, and they felt rough against her tongue. She ate them anyway.

Gino watched her as if he couldn't quite believe what he was seeing.

In her torn and filthy nylon shorts, equally tattered bikini top, bare feet dirty and bloody in Natalie's sandals, her short hair mussed and matted, her face and body muddy and scratched and blood-stained, she looked like a crazed feral animal.

"Quinn," he said softly, "where's everyone else?"

"There is no everyone else."

"Jesus." Gino's sweat-slick face twisted into a grimace. "Jesus Christ." He bowed his head. When he looked up again, his eyes were moist. "I—I failed you. I failed all of you. I'm sorry."

"None of that matters now."

"I tried to get up," he said. "I—I tried, Quinn, but I—I can't feel my leg anymore."

"I did the best I could," she told him. "It's bad."

"I know, I..."

His voice trailed off, and they were quiet for a while, helpless in the silence.

"This thing," Quinn finally said, "it uses the tunnels. It hides in them, moves through them to get from one part of the island to another. I think it sleeps down there too. If it sleeps."

"What the hell is it?"

"I'm not sure. But if we have any chance at all, we can't wait for it to come to us again. I have to be the predator now."

"Quinn—"

"It's the only way." She gathered up the four grenades they'd found and placed two next to him. "If I don't make it, use these."

As Gino struggled to remain conscious, Quinn remembered the dream, holding her husband's hand as birds fell from the sky in flames.

"I'm going after it. Down into those tunnels."

"And then what?"

"I'll kill it."

"How?"

"With the one thing that kills everything," she said. "*Fire.*"

CHAPTER FIFTEEN

Beneath an unforgiving sun, through the blur of heat rising up off the island, her skin scarred and sunburned, battered and bathed in sweat, Quinn stood at the entrance to the tunnels. Having armed herself with the ax and two grenades, she'd ventured back into the jungle and down the slope where she'd fallen, this time negotiating the terrain slowly and carefully, until she'd reached the opening in the ground the creature had last vanished into.

Sitting on the edge, she drew a deep breath then slid down into the hole.

It was a drop of several feet, and as she landed, her knees buckled and she found herself sitting on the dirt floor. Before her, the tunnel. And darkness.

The tunnel was just deep enough for her to stand in, but the creature was too tall to be completely upright here. She envisioned it crouched over, moving rapidly through the dirt and darkness, imagined it hidden in the shadows just ahead, waiting for her. Breathing heavily, Quinn pressed forward.

The light from above was still evident, but within seconds it was well behind her and she found herself in total darkness. With each step, perspective became more and more of a challenge, and it was increasingly difficult to differentiate up from down.

She stopped a moment and listened. Air dirty and stale filled her lungs. It was decidedly cooler but terribly claustrophobic beneath the earth, and the tunnel was far narrower than she'd expected it to be. She could touch the dirt walls on either side of her without fully extending her arms. Even had she wanted to, there wasn't sufficient room to do so. Placing a hand against the side of the tunnel for balance and some sense of where she was, Quinn crept forward. Eyes wide and straining to see something—anything—the darkness conspired with the close tunnel walls and low ceiling to leave her not only blind but feeling like everything was constricting, closing in and strangling her. The uneven terrain only made it worse, and the deeper she went, the more claustrophobic she became.

Following the curve of the wall with her hand pressed flat against it, Quinn felt the tunnel changing direction once, then twice, winding through the underground passages beneath the island like some giant ant farm. She couldn't tell for sure but she'd gone several hundred yards and been in complete darkness for several minutes, when something in the distance caught her eye.

Bleeding through the darkness, a light. A flame. Flickering.

She stopped, leaned against the side of the tunnel. Waited.

Listened.

Nothing.

Until that awful smell reached her.

The creature was close.

Heart pounding, Quinn gripped the ax tighter and, quietly as she could, moved toward the light. The Japanese hand grenades, unlike the American versions she'd seen in photographs and movies, were squat, with something of a square shape, but outfitted with a typical serrated design which gave them a pineapple-like appearance. Clipped to the waistband of her shorts, the fuse pins were faced outward and away from her body. She reached down and touched them quickly to make sure neither had fallen free, then continued on.

The tunnel narrowed even further, and suddenly emptied into a small chamber. Though the flame was still a good distance away, it provided enough light for her to see glimpses of the uneven floors, and some of the debris that had found its way down there over the decades: dead vegetation and leaves, a good deal of rocks and branches, and the bones of small rodents and even a few birds and bats. Once she'd reached the end of the chamber, Quinn crawled into another narrow passageway.

Light bled closer, filling the darkness.

She stopped, remained hidden in the shadows just beyond its reach. Before her, a larger circular chamber with the same low ceilings but a much wider and open area. On the walls, wood sconces had been positioned every few feet, all the torches within them long extinguished, but for the one burning bright and strong.

My God, she thought, *this thing has fire.*

Her eyes followed the shadows and pool of flickering light to the chamber floor.

It too was littered with bones. But these were mostly human. Skulls, purposely constructed into piles or simply strewn about like garbage.

Like an old open grave, the smell of death was strong in this terrible place.

The fire crackled, the light dancing across the dirt walls and the curve of the low ceiling. But it was the rest of what the fire revealed that left Quinn wracked with fear. Shaking uncontrollably, she breathed quietly as possible, frozen in terror.

A throne-like chair constructed from human and animal bones sat in the center of the chamber, the creature sitting atop it, eyes closed, the sword laying across its knees and its arms folded across its chest. The throne was adorned with mummified human hands and other body parts, and at the creature's feet, two piles of human skulls sat on either side of him. Still as a corpse, the thing sat upon its chair, the flame bathing it in an eerie orange glow.

Maybe it does sleep after all, Quinn thought.

Her blood ran cold. Remaining where she was, she watched the thing a while.

It seemed unaware of her presence, and had neither opened its eyes nor moved since she'd come upon it. She couldn't be certain, but it didn't appear to be breathing.

What the hell was this thing? What in God's name was she dealing with?

But there, in the dark, she knew. She knew.

All these years it had waited here, in its kingdom of blood and bone and death, sitting atop its throne deep beneath the earth, a profane abomination conjured from evil born of the darkest corners of existence. Brought forth to wage destruction on anything or anyone that crossed its path, that dared enter its realm—this godforsaken island—it had slithered out from the shadows of Hell to protect this house of horrors from any and all intruders. An ancient and deadly warrior, an evil spirit made whole through rituals of blood and horror, torture, sorrow, unimaginable pain and murder, this was an entity of pure vengeance that would stop at nothing to fulfill its dark and twisted destiny.

She'd been wrong all along. There *was* such a thing as monsters.

Steeling herself, Quinn stepped into the chamber, into the light. At her feet, more skulls and mummified body parts. But one stopped her dead.

Her husband's severed head lay among them, his dead eyes still open.

Rage, horror and sorrow exploded, churning deep inside her like a dust devil. All sanity was gone in that nightmare moment. She was nothing but a rabid, dangerous predator now, the same savage that had killed Herm.

With furious anger, Quinn stepped around the skulls and closed on the throne.

The thing opened its red eyes.

She swung the ax with every bit of strength she possessed.

The creature raised an arm to block the blow, but the blade hit it in the shoulder. Bringing it back around, she crashed the ax into the thing again, and this time it did damage, smashing the armor along its left arm and shoulder.

Stumbling on the follow-through and off-balance, Quinn quickly righted herself.

With a disturbing creaking sound, the creature rose from its throne, the metal armor clacking as it stepped down and leveled its sword at her.

Herm's bald head fell free from its lap and rolled into darkness, as Quinn swung again, this time for its massive chest. It connected, knocking the being back, but only a few steps. Seemingly unaffected, it looked at her with its horrible crimson eyes, cocking its head as if baffled by her attack.

Then it lunged for her.

Wheeling away into the shadows from which she'd come, Quinn scrambled for the passageway. Turning back, she pulled a grenade free of her waistband, yanked the pin out and rolled it along the dirt floor toward the throne.

248

GREG F. GIFUNE

It came to a stop at the samurai's feet. The creature looked down at it, as if unsure of what it was.

Quinn dropped, rolled away into darkness and braced herself.

But no explosion came.

The thing stalked across the chamber after her. The grenade was a dud. Were it going to work, it would've by then. Maybe they were too old to detonate, or maybe she'd simply gotten one that malfunctioned, she couldn't know for sure. All she *did* know, was that her plan had backfired, and the creature was closing on her.

Standing, she swung the ax again, but missed.

The creature responded with a backhand that connected with the side of Quinn's head and took her off her feet.

She flew across the chamber, landing hard on her back, several feet away near the entrance to the passageway.

Jaw aching and head spinning, she retreated into the tunnels, stumbling back into the pitch-black as fast as her legs would carry her. Enveloped again in darkness absolute, she had no idea in which direction she was headed. Her only hope was that she'd gotten it right, that she'd emerge from the tunnels at least close to where she'd planned to, but there was no time to reconsider, no way to be certain. The only thing she was aware of in those terrifying moments was her instinctual need for flight.

She vaulted through the narrow tunnels.

The creature gave chase.

Lost in darkness and dizzy from the blow to her head, all sense of place and time abandoned her. She felt as if she were freefalling through an empty black void with no beginning or end, an astronaut broken free of her tether, tumbling away through a dark expanse of deep, endless space.

And then she smelled something above the creature's nauseating stench.

Fresh air.

Something behind her brushed her bare leg, and she screamed out but never slowed her pace, throwing herself through the tunnel. To her left—light—a small hole of it punched in the darkness just up ahead. She hurried toward it, the sounds of the creature's footfalls trailing close behind her.

Quinn saw the opening well before she'd reached it, and prepared herself for what she had to do. Once within reach of it, without slowing, she jumped, launching herself up and through the tunnel opening. As she emerged, exploding into the daylight, she threw the ax out ahead of her and quickly grabbed the ground on either side of the hole, struggling to pull herself up before sliding back down into the tunnel.

Snatching at vines and anything else she could get hold of, Quinn kicked with her legs and pulled with her arms, struggling up and out.

A cold dead hand clamped onto her ankle with tremendous force.

Halfway out of the opening now, she kicked with her free leg as hard as she could. Once. Twice. A third time, and then a fourth. Each blow connected with the being, but it felt as if she were kicking a cement wall. By the fifth kick, the hand released her, sliding down and tearing the sandal from her foot as Quinn crawled the rest of the way out and scrambled for the ax.

The last grenade she had fell free. She reached back for it just as the creature emerged. Snatching it up, she regained her feet and took off through the jungle, unsure of where she was on the island.

Everything flew past her in a frantic blur.

With only one sandal on, her gait was uneven and awkward, so she hopped a few steps, pulled the other sandal off, tossed it aside and broke back into a full run. Ignoring the pain blasting into the soles of her feet, the burning in her lungs, the aches and soreness throughout her body, the slightly blurred vision and throbbing in her jaw and head, she sped through the jungle. What little she could make sense of didn't help, because wherever she was, this part of the island did not look familiar at all.

Moving up and over an incline, she came to a halt and looked back. Not far behind her, walking rather than running through the jungle, its stride steady and purposeful, came the spirit warrior, an impossible demon of aged iron and decayed flesh, worn leather and tarnished metal, steel horns and fiery, subhuman eyes.

Quinn ran. Without any idea where she was or where she was

headed, she ran.

She raised the ax and held it out in front of her, hoping to shield her eyes and block some of the sharper vines and branches stabbing at her as she crashed through the jungle. Pure adrenaline increased her speed, and as she closed on a particularly thick area of brush, she jumped into the air in an attempt to burst through it without having to slow down.

Her body punched through, the jungle tore open and she sailed into the air.

Suddenly there was nothing but vast and beautiful sky before her. The ground was no more, and though she was still running, it was in midair, flailing.

And then she began to fall.

It wasn't until she plummeted down and crashed into the ground that she realized she'd run right off the edge of a precipice, the literal end of one side of the island, and was now tumbling and rolling violently down the severely slanted, rocky and vine-covered terrain. With astounding velocity, she bounced along, occasionally finding air only to crash back to earth and tumble further down, the air forced from her lungs, her grip on the ax lost. Barely conscious, she bounced and slammed down the side of the crag for what seemed an eternity, finally splashing down into some wet sand along a small and narrow stretch of beach.

Quinn lay there a moment, unable to move.

From somewhere above, there came a deafening blast that shook the ground beneath her and sent dirt, rocks and debris showering down all around her.

Turtling, she covered her head, waiting until the rain had ceased.

Slowly, the pain returned, moving through, searing and tearing at her as with tremendous effort, Quinn pushed herself up to her knees. Spitting dirt and grass from her mouth, she looked around, tried to get her bearings and clear her head. After a few seconds, she realized where she was, and what happened.

She'd fallen all the way down to the ocean, and on the way, the grenade in her waistband had come free and detonated, leaving a crater in the side of the crag about one hundred yards above her.

Of course, she thought, *that one fucking worked.*

Her arms, legs and feet were badly scraped, scratched and bleeding from several small wounds, and she'd bitten her tongue and smashed her nose as well, so they too were bleeding. But somehow, far as she could tell, she'd managed to survive the fall without any serious injuries.

Back on her feet, she swayed and her knees buckled, dropping her back to the wet sand. Looking up the side of the cliff, she saw no sign of the creature.

Quinn tried to stand again. This time her legs held her.

Frantically, she looked for the ax. It was gone.

A small rockslide began, peppering the narrow shoreline with debris from the side of the cliff.

Quinn looked up.

The thing was coming. Running down the side of the cliff, sword drawn.

Nothing human could do that.

Following the rocky base of the cliff, Quinn hurried along the small stretch of sand then climbed up and over a small embankment and back into the jungle. She'd not been here before, but knew now roughly where she must be.

As the creature dropped the final length of cliff, the bottoms of its booted feet slamming into the wet sand in an explosion of dirt, water and blood, pieces of its damaged armor falling away, Quinn ran.

She had virtually nothing left. Exhausted and battered, she no longer had the strength to run with any real speed, but she kept moving anyway, allowing raw instinct and adrenaline to carry her.

As she staggered through the jungle, hoping she was headed in the right direction, she made her way steadily through the difficult terrain, her bare feet torn and scraped. Every step agonizing, she hobbled along. There was only survival. Only the will to live. To beat this thing. To kill it for all it had done to them. To her.

It was not love that drove her, but hatred.

Drenched in sweat, Quinn finally reached the clearing. Nearly breaking down, she pushed her emotions aside and stumbled into the outpost.

She fell near the flagpole, which still displayed the bodies of her friends.

Rather than look, she struggled back to her feet and ran to the edge of the tunnel she'd emptied the drums of gasoline into. She could smell it, the fumes wafting about in the thick hot air.

In the doorway to the officer's quarters, stood Gino, propped up and using a rifle as a crutch. He looked near death, coughing and pale and covered in sweat. But he'd seen her, and called her name.

Why was he calling her name when she was so close?

And then she realized it was because the creature was coming up behind her.

She turned in time to see it closing on her.

Throwing herself to the ground, she avoided the blade of its sword as it rushed past, but as she rolled away and lay on her back, she saw it was still coming for her, moving toward her with that same deliberate walk.

She wanted to get up. The voice in her head screamed for her to get up, to fight.

But she couldn't. Even if she tried, she wouldn't make it back to her feet in time. It was already standing over her, the sword raised, the blade glistening and catching the sun with profane beauty.

Quinn closed her eyes.

Someone was screaming.

Gino. Screaming to it at the top of his lungs, with everything he had left.

She opened her eyes. Though barely visible in the glaring sun, she could see it had straddled her and raised its sword. But Gino's screams continued, and rather than finish her off, it turned, left her, and started toward him.

Get up, she thought. *Get—Get up, get—up.*

Something landed on the ground next to her, bounced and rolled close. Quinn sat up, shielding her eyes from the sun. A grenade. Gino had thrown her one of the grenades she'd left with him.

As she snatched it up, Gino screamed again. But this was different.

The thing had stabbed him clean through. A long section of blade protruded grotesquely from Gino's back. Screaming again, he gagged on his own blood, dropping the rifle as the creature lifted him off the ground and high into the air, driving the sword even deeper.

Gino's limp body slid down until the entire blade was inside him up to the handle. The creature's blood-soaked hands had penetrated him as well.

Quinn pushed herself up onto her feet, but she was so weak she could barely hold her balance. "Gino," she heard herself say.

As blood exploded from his mouth and nose, running down his face and spraying the creature, Gino began to laugh. It was a gurgling, horrible sound that quickly turned to a gagging cough, but he raised his hands just before he died, and Quinn knew then what he was telling her.

In one hand he held a grenade. In the other, the fuse pin.

The explosion rocked the entire outpost, and knocked Quinn back off her feet. All around her, dirt and debris flew up and showered down as she hit the ground, her ears ringing and all sound muffled and distant.

The blast launched both Gino and the creature off the porch and onto the ground several feet away.

In pieces. Bloody, horrific pieces.

And then, unnatural silence.

Soon, a buzzing sound rang in Quinn's ears. It became a rumble, before finally, gradually, her hearing returned to normal.

Her vision still blurred, she pawed at her eyes.

The explosion had caused the front of the building to catch fire. It burned, slowly but steadily, climbing the walls and running along the remains of the porch.

Quinn forced herself to look at the bodies. They lay together, in a tangled bloody heap. It was difficult to tell where the creature ended and Gino began, and while they were largely intact, body parts and viscera lay scattered around them, including one of Gino's legs, which had landed several feet away.

Gino had saved her life.

Or so she thought.

Until what remained of the creature slowly rose from the carnage.

A bloody stump of bone was all that remained where the thing's right arm had been. It's armor, tattered and missing in many places, hung on the creature now, and its helmet had been knocked free, leaving only the leather faceplate that covered everything below its eyes. Its head was covered in scars and nearly bald, but for a few long sprigs of black hair dangling grotesquely from it. In the blast it had sustained an enormous wound in its side, and a large chunk had been blown out of one of its thighs. Slowly, it reached up with its only hand, ripped its faceplate free and threw it aside.

Its face was hideous, horribly scarred and leathery, a patchwork of decayed and mummified flesh that appeared to have been sewn together by disciples of Doctor Frankenstein. The nose was skeletal, and the mouth had no lips, just a badly scarred and revolting slash of an opening, behind which, teeth black as coal resided.

It shook free of its armor. The metal panels and mesh material fell to the ground in a heap. Beneath it the creature wore what remained of a cloth tunic. It watched her with its red eyes, as if it were trying to understand.

Their eyes remained locked, and in those few seconds, Quinn swore she saw something more. Something akin to respect in those bloody eyes, as if it had deemed her worthy somehow.

"Come get me," she said, her voice rough and raw, foreign even to her. "I'm not running anymore."

The creature looked to the ground, searching for its sword.

258

Still clutching the grenade, Quinn crawled to the entrance of the tunnels just as it located its weapon and drew it free from the pile of Gino's remains. The sword, slick and drenched, dripped with blood and bodily fluids.

A tongue, black and diseased looking, emerged from the creature's horrific mouth. Slowly, it brought the blade to its face, licked it clean then let out a guttural, rumbling laugh.

When it again fell silent, Quinn managed to get herself up into a crouched position.

The thing swung its sword about, quickly and out before it, as if to showcase its skills, and then with an inhuman screech, a war cry of death and destruction, it vaulted toward her.

Quinn pushed off with everything she had, rocketing herself up and straight at it.

Her shoulder crashed into its midsection. She bounced off and rolled away, but the force of the contact knocked the thing off balance, and it toppled into the hole, falling and sliding down into the tunnels.

Scrambling back to the tunnel opening, Quinn saw it laying in the dirt below, its legs bent at impossible angles. Yet it continued to struggle to stand, to come for her. A heartless killing machine of spirit, flesh, blood and bone, it would not stop, *could* not stop. Not ever.

"Die," she growled through gritted teeth. "*Die.*"

Looking once more into its terrible eyes, Quinn pulled the pin and dropped the grenade down on top of the creature.

Crippled and still on its back, the thing continued to struggle to stand.

Quinn ran for the lagoon.

The explosion was massive, as the gasoline ignited as well, shooting fire up and out of the hole while also surging through the tunnels. The flames rocketed beneath the earth, exploding out through several exits and catching the surrounding areas on fire.

Knocked to the ground, Quinn lay just beyond the outpost.

Amidst the dirt, debris and flames, pieces of the ancient warrior fell like rain all around her. The fire had spread, and the flames and sparks falling from the initial explosion ignited the other buildings as well.

Soon, the fire had reached the surrounding jungle.

A bloody and battered mess, Quinn lay trembling uncontrollably, the final look in the demon's eyes still burned into her vision.

She fell still and slipped away to unconsciousness. Or something similar.

She dreamed of death. Blood. Carnage. Tears.

And fire.

She dreamed of moving through the tunnels, the darkness,

the island above her consumed in flames and smoke. She dreamed of burrowing even deeper into the earth, so many bloody skulls cradled in her arms.

Howling winds echoed in her mind, screaming like animals being slaughtered.

Finally, she dreamed of nothing at all. Darkness, empty and endless.

A void from which no one ever fully returned.

When Quinn awakened, she was no longer afraid. The fire continued to spread, and by nightfall, the entire island had become an inferno. She removed the tattered remnants of her clothing, and using a finger, decorated her face with her own blood, marking it like a warrior using war paint. Like the predator she'd become.

Then she sat back and watched the world burn.

AFTER

It was quite an impressive spread. Hot coffee, tea, various drinks, numerous fresh fruits and plates of steaming breakfast foods—scrambled eggs and bacon and sausage, corn beef hash, hash browns, and all of it displayed across a large table covered in beautiful white linen. The tent, under which a large rug, table and chairs had been placed, was brightly colored and ornate, outfitted with rows of lights and torches on either side of the entrance that burned bright once the sun went down. But it was early morning, and the sun was still rising over the clear blue ocean, the tent positioned on a gorgeous section of beach just walking distance from their hotel.

Everyone looked amazing. Healthy and rested, tan and vibrant.

Even Herm, who was in the middle of a story about one of his students, looked good, not so pasty and disheveled.

They ate their breakfasts and drank their coffee and tea, laughing and joking with each other, enjoying their vacation. And this resort, so beautiful it just got better and better, beyond anything they'd hoped for.

"I don't think I ever want to go home," Quinn said.

Dallas raised his juice glass. "I'll drink to that."

"Hell yeah, I could go for beach bumming it here the rest of my life," Andre said.

"Have you ever seen a more beautiful sunrise?" Natalie asked through a bright smile. "I'm in love with this place."

Gino ate like he always did, purposefully, steadily. Not too fast, not too slowly. Unlike the others, he didn't engage in conversation much as he normally did, but laughed when it was appropriate and seemed to be thoroughly enjoying himself.

Quinn reached over, touched her husband's hand and smiled at him.

Dallas gave her a wink and popped a piece of bacon in his mouth.

Wake up.

"Okay, so anyway," Herm said, continuing his story and chuckling around a mouthful of eggs and sausage. "The test question was, in 1803 the United States purchased land from the French, and President Jefferson chose two men to travel to this unexplored land and report back to him what they found. What were the names of the explorers he chose for this historic expedition? And the kid says…"

They all waited.

"Martin and Lewis?"

Everyone laughed. Except for Harper, who seemed even more

confused than usual, which was saying something.

"I don't get it," she whined. "Who's Marvin and Lewis?"

Gino was the only one able to contain himself. Everyone else's laughter only got worse, and Herm nearly choked he was laughing so hard.

"Jesus Christ, babe." Gino sighed. "You know who Lewis and Clark are, right? The explorers? The kid should've said Lewis and Clark. That was right answer."

"Um…'kay…so…who's Marvin and Lewis then?"

"*Martin* and Lewis," he said, dropping his fork.

Andre was laughing so hard he was crying.

Gino shot him a helpless look then turned back to Harper. "They were a comedy team. You know, Dean Martin and Jerry Lewis?"

"Who? *God*, why is everything you guys talk about so confusing?"

Quinn got up from the table, a cup of coffee in hand, and walked across the rug to the sand, and out of the tent. She was laughing too, but felt bad, and saw no reason to be mean to Harper. Quinn never understood deliberate cruelty, and wanted no part of it, even when it was meant to be funny and harmless. Harper was young, vacuous and very limited, but she seemed like a nice enough kid.

Kid, Quinn thought. *Now she's a kid. What does that make me?*

The ocean breeze rolled in slowly, seductively. Quinn loved the way it felt in her hair, against her face, and couldn't recall ever having been quite so content.

Her bare foot brushed against something partially buried in the sand.

An old LIFE magazine…

Tell us what you see.

A young Katherine Hepburn on the cover.

Wake up now, Quinn. It's time to wake up and tell us your secrets.

Another outburst of laughter drew her attention back to the tent.

Wake up.

She looked back over her shoulder at the others. They were no longer laughing, but staring at her instead, their faces sullen, wet and dripping blood.

Tears filled her eyes, blurred the horrific scene and rolled across her cheeks.

Wake up, Quinn. Wake up.

The fire was what brought them. The island burned for hours, the fire sweeping through the jungle to create an enormous beacon in the night, in a stretch of ocean thought to be void of any land whatsoever.

She knew they were there. She'd seen them approaching, several of them leaving the larger vessel anchored beyond the reef and taking a smaller boat to the beach. She counted eight in all. *Strange*, she thought. *There were eight of us.*

As they stood on the beach, their flashlights unnecessary with most of the island still ablaze, she wasn't sure if she should approach them or not. She couldn't be sure anymore if leaving this place was good or bad.

Good, she finally decided, *but…*

She was not the same as before. She never could be.

Moving with stealth and precision, she crept from the tunnels to the sand.

They hadn't seen her yet. They wouldn't until she allowed it.

Her head hurt and it was still difficult to sort her thoughts. But she knew she wanted her husband…she…she wanted Dallas but…he was no more.

Neither am I, she thought.

Slowly, she walked along the waterline, the saltwater so cool and healing against her bloody feet.

Monstrous waves of heat surged and pulsed from the fiery jungle, a giant furnace blasting directly at her. But there was something beautiful about it. So pure.

"Dear God!" a male voice bellowed.

She'd gotten within reach of them before they even realized she was there.

Only one was a woman, and at closer range she saw they were

all wearing matching uniforms. Shocked to see her standing there, one man asked, "What the hell happened here?"

The woman held a blanket, and when no answer was given, she approached cautiously. "Ma' am? It's all right, we're not going to hurt you."

You can't hurt me.

"It's all right," the woman told her again. "Do you understand? It's all right, we're here to help you."

She remained still. Nude and battered and covered in blood and soot, she no longer had any shame or concern for such things. This was her island. She'd killed for it. Many had died for it.

"Are you alone?" the woman asked. "Is there anyone else here with you?"

You wouldn't understand even if I told you. There are many here. In the trees...in the sand and rock...in the fire...in the lone building that still stands deep in the jungle.

"Are you alone?" the woman pressed.

They're all around us...

"Are you...Are you the only one left?"

She nodded.

"Can you tell me your name?"

Yes. But I'm not going to.

"It's okay," the woman said, "that doesn't matter now. We're going to get you home. Do you understand? It's over, we've found you, it's all over. We're going to get you home."

I am home...

"Do you understand what I'm telling you?" the woman asked. "I want you to come with us now, all right? We're going to take you home."

The woman stepped closer and carefully wrapped the blanket around her, then gently guided her toward the others and the waiting boat.

She easily could've killed each one of them had she wanted to. These fools, these children, they'd never know what hit them.

But rather than attack, she went with them instead. Why, she wasn't quite sure.

Perhaps somewhere deep inside her there still existed a shred of the thoughtful and gentle woman who would've collapsed and cried at such a miraculous rescue. Perhaps one day she'd even be able to conjure that person again and bring her back to life. Like a corpse long cold from the grave.

For now, there was only fire...death...suffering.

And nightmares. *Torturous* nightmares.

As they led her into the ocean and onto the small boat, she looked back one last time at the inferno behind her, and the remnants of this awful place that had both cost and given her so much.

Her eyes burned fire-red.

Or perhaps they were just reflecting the endless flames.

There was really no way to know for sure.

Not yet.

THE END

ABOUT THE AUTHOR

Greg F. Gifune is a best-selling, internationally-published author of several acclaimed novels, novellas and two short story collections. Called, "The best writer of horror and supernatural thrillers at work today" by New York Times best-selling author Christopher Rice, "One of the best writers of his generation" by both The Roswell Literary Review and author Brian Keene, and "Among the finest dark suspense writers of our time" by legendary best-selling author Ed Gorman, Greg's work has been published all over the world, translated into several languages, received starred reviews from Publishers Weekly, Library Journal, Kirkus and others, is consistently praised by readers and critics alike, and has garnered attention from Hollywood. His novel THE BLEEDING SEASON, originally published in 2003, has been hailed as a classic in the genre and is considered to be one of the best horror/thriller novels of the decade. In 2016 his short stories HOAX and PLANT LIFE will be adapted to film. Also an editor with years of experience in the field in a variety of positions, Greg is presently on hiatus from his position as Senior Editor at DarkFuse, and at work on several projects. He resides in Massachusetts with his wife Carol, a bevy of cats and two dogs, Dozer and Bella. He can be reached online at gfgauthor@verizon.net or on Facebook and Twitter.

Made in the USA
Monee, IL
07 August 2021